OUTSIDERS WITHIN

OUTSIDERS WITHIN

Edited by

Dave Higgins

And featuring stories by
Joel Donato Jacob
dave ring
Willow Croft
Ryan Priest
Noah Lemelson
Lillian Csernica
Samantha Bryant
Christopher Maleney
M.R. Blackmoor
Jonathan Titchenal
Glenn A. Bruce
Dave Higgins

CONTENTS

INTRODUCTION

I first encountered Lovecraft's work as a young teenager. Someone in my class brought a collection to school and claimed it was great. My small local library didn't have any Lovecraft so I forgot about him and moved on; however, months later while seeking something to read on a trip to visit my father, I saw Granada Publishing's *At the Mountains of Madness and Other Novels of Terror* omnibus and was tempted. I loved it so much that I not only finished it within a couple of days but scoured the bookshops near my father's house for the next omnibus in the series.

Unsurprisingly for someone who started with *At the Mountains of Madness* (rather than one of Lovecraft's shorter or more accessible works) and wasn't put off, I've been reading and rereading Lovecraft every since, along with a steadily expanding collection of authors who crafted their own perspectives on cosmicism. So, I've had the idea of publishing my own cosmic horror anthology in the back of mind almost as long as the idea of being a publisher.

But all those books also reminded me that each author's viewpoint on what is cosmic horror is a tiny island in a vast black sea of possibilities; so I'd need a theme to prevent the anthology being disassociated stories each straining in their own direction.

I found inspiration in the one thing all cosmic horror shares: the discovery that an incomprehensible otherness lurks beneath the thin veneer of humanity's beliefs in order and purpose, that there are secrets which will tear apart our comfortable lives. Instead of limiting the focus to particular regions, times, or genre-tropes, I'd seek stories where the protagonists had their own secret.

Something embarrassing, shameful, even criminal. Something they hid beneath a veneer of being an ordinary member of their society.

Appropriately, reading the submissions eroded my belief in the tidiness of my theme: as well as protagonists with mundane secrets discovering new horrors, I found people who had already encountered the irrational and had their reaction to it shaped by their own secrets; and situations where the protagonist perceived an underlying reality but the reader was left in the position of someone only hearing the story, having to decide whether the protagonist's view was real or delusion.

My own contribution sprang from a joke about needing to put my stamp on the anthology.

Some of these stories show their Lovecraftian roots openly, others resonate with the concepts but not the names. Some are bleaker than others. But each of them shows someone who is both outside and within a world that isn't the firm foundation they thought.

—Dave Higgins, November 2020

THE FRACTURE FOR SALVADOR MIGUEL

JOEL DONATO JACOB

Salvador Miguel had to duck into the Indio chief's hut to see Lana, the boy groomed to be sacrificed to appease the hunger of Naga, the sky serpent. The missionary from Spain was already head and shoulders taller than the primitives but the natives also liked to hang tools, crops, and nests for egg-laying chickens from the roof beams. The natives sorely needed the guidance of the Empire. Plowshares threatened to cut the unwary and those fowl droppings probably caused the many afflictions that plagued the land.

Yet even in the dreadful circumstances, Salvador Miguel found himself basking in the radiance of Lana. The boy was raised from birth for this role.

Lana was never allowed to touch soil, nor was sunlight ever allowed to touch his skin. He was fair like a European, silky skinned and soft-featured. His hands were slender and ended in pearly fingertips. Lana's mouth was typical of an Indio, thick and wide, but they were the color of fresh blood, while the typical Indio's were the color of scab. Having never seen the sun's glare, Lana's eyes were so black that Salvador Miguel would often lose himself in them looking for the distinction of irises.

Lana became aware of his visitor even as two handmaidens were brushing coconut oil into hair that had never been cut. Two servants were sewing the ritual costume onto his body closed. He was schedule to die in the beaded and embroidered jacket and skirt. He was probably going to be buried in them too. Lana no longer needed the convenience of doffing them.

Seemingly overcome with bashfulness at his partial state of undress, Lana looked into the fire pit in the center of the hut. His eyes reflected the flames briefly even as he blinked the smile budding in his lips away. Composed, Lana raised his chin and greeted Salvador Miguel with a nod.

Salvador Miguel caught himself smiling because of the smile that he did not receive.

"Could we get some privacy?"

Lana slowly panned his gaze about the room. "What do you mean? There is no one else here!"

Salvador Miguel had forgotten that in their primitive caste system, it was unbecoming for someone from the ruling Maginoo class to acknowledge the existence of their slaves. It was considered rude to assume that the servants did not serve so absolutely and perfectly, like air, anticipating the masters' whims and needs even as surely as water flowed down. Once the Empire of Spain was done bringing civilization to these lands, these slaves would be emancipated. But that was a concern for a brighter day.

There was darkness upon them and Salvador Miguel must act.

"I have convinced the Capitan to use the force of the Constabulario to liberate you."

There was a flash of concern that briefly knitted Lana's brows together but they unraveled just as quickly.

"You will do no such thing." Lana tried to laugh but he could not mask the worry in his voice.

Salvador Miguel wondered if Lana doubted they would succeed. "There is so much beauty in the world that you have yet to experience. I... I will take you to Europe with me. There is a boat on the bay that will sail tonight. You will be in Spain in time for the first snow. They sparkle like your eyes; they are delicate like your touch."

"There is so much beauty in the world and I have the honor of making sure that this beauty will still be there tomorrow."

Salvador Miguel was almost taken aback. Lana was the single most educated Indio he had met. Raised in seclusion, Lana had the leisure of time to learn to read Arabic, Chinese, and eventually Spanish. Salvador Miguel was outraged that he could be so ignorant.

"There are libraries larger than this entire village in Madrid, more poetry than you can ever memorize." Salvador Miguel loved every moment of the day-long epics that Lana was forced to memorize and recite them at will. "Poetry will be written about you."

"There will be poetry a-plenty in the festivities tonight. You may sing me praises then."

"Is there no reasoning with you?"

"There is a reason, Salvador Miguel."

Was that coyness in his voice? Salvador Miguel wondered with the incredulity. He was trying to save Lana's life and he dared to condescend.

"I want you to live."

"I want my people to live."

Salvador Miguel suppressed his outrage. Lana was just misled by his heretic faith.

Salvador Miguel stood up to his full height and loomed over Lana and his attendants where they sat in the hut. The missionary grabbed Lana by the wrist and pulled him to his feet and dragged him out of the hut. The Spaniard had to duck and weave to dodge the low hanging farm implements and drying crops. When he looked back, Lana flowed through the obstructions smoothly like water. He was still radiant, graceful, despite his sinful nature and the sins he evoked in others. This sacrifice must be stopped.

Lana's attendants rushed ahead of them and Salvador Miguel worried that they were going to warn the village of his plans. But Salvador Miguel knew that the Guardia of the Constabulario waited outside, armed with their rifles.

Salvador Miguel was expecting the familiar pops of rifles but there were none. He stepped out of the hut to see the former convicts, acquitted to perform the Lord's divine mission of bringing his grace to the ignorant savages, aiming their rifles at the ground. Some were scanning the rice paddies between the chief's hut and the village square for intruders. The moon over the horizon, full and huge revealed that there were none. Everything was cast in a pale yellow, like unflickering candlelight. The sound of celebration a few hundred paces away carried in the still wind as drink containers clattered and the sound of merriment. Salvador Miguel all but loathed the savages for celebrating a sacrifice of such a beautiful being of God's creation as Lana.

Instead of making a run for it, the Indio slaves had prostrated themselves upon the ground beyond the short flight of stairs that lead up to the Village Chiefs hut.

Salvador stepped over them. He wondered what they were doing until he saw Lana step on them. Lana could not step on soil and the slaves were obligated to make sure of that. Even as Lana's foot left the back of a slave, they would scramble up and rush forward to keep Lana's feet off the ground. Frustrated by the whirl of running slaves, Salvador Miguel picked Lana up and cradled the Indio boy in his arms.

Lana was light, as if his bones were hollow like a bird's, even as Salvador Miguel felt the muscles under the skin that let the Indio move with like a leaf on the breeze when he danced.

The Constabulario guards flanked Salvador Miguel as he walked towards the River Pasig where the small boat will take them to Manila Bay. There, the galleon Sofia la Amada was waiting to take them to Spain. Salvador Miguel hated this look upon Lana's face, as if he loathed him, but the Indio's body betrayed him, he did not struggle in his arms. Lana could have easily made a run for it, but he didn't. Surely, Miguel Salvador wondered, Lana knew this whole thing with never touching the soil was but some pagan superstition.

"It begins." Lana's gaze had been stuck on the uneven horizon, where the mountain ranges that nestled his village met the sky, since they left the chief's hut. Miguel Salvador saw his face brighten.

Joy. Miguel Salvador looked up jealously to see what could bring joy to Lana's face when he had never and could not.

It was the moon. Miguel Salvador corrected himself. It was not just the moon. A shadow had started to crawl over the face of the moon.

This must be their Sky Serpent, Naga. It was just an eclipse after all. The pagans were fools as well as sinners.

The shadow crept across the landscape. Square by square the paddies blinked out of view. Salvador felt Lana's gaze shift. When he looked, the Indio gazed up, instead of the eclipse happening before his eyes.

Curious, Salvador Miguel also looked up just as the last sliver of moon winked out of sight. The world was enveloped in darkness and all the stars winked into view. Lana was looking at a strip of nebulous glow across the night sky. It was the Milky Way, Salvador Miguel could see how these natives could think that the edge of our known galaxy was the belly of some humongous celestial snake wrapped around the world. In a way, Salvador Miguel pitied Lana for his ignorance.

Then the belly of the Sky Serpent heaved and the sky above them cracked. Thunderous noise erupted overhead even as the sound of panicked screaming can be heard from the celebrations in the distance. The Constabulario guards, hardened criminals each, started praying their Ave Marias and Nuestro Padres.

Bits of the sky broke and crashed into the paddies and the mountains. Clear panes of crystal, no one would mistake them for meteorites.

Nothing about this made sense to Salvador Miguel. He prayed to the God of the Jews, Christians, and Muslims; but he also prayed to Science and Logic, powers he held to as high a regarded as Gods. He had faith in the laws of physics, dependable and constant, replicable, unlike miracles.

Lana, from Salvador Miguel embracing arms, lifts his hands into the night sky as huge cracks combine into a breach into space. The moon had reappeared in the horizon but its brightness does not diminish the starry belly of Naga.

The Sky Serpent slithers through the gap he had made in the sky and lowers his head towards the valley where Salvador Miguel still carried Lana. The Constabulario had run away in panic. In the distance, the Indios could be heard begging for forgiveness that their tribute had been stolen.

Salvador Miguel dropped Lana and ran for his life.

When the Spaniard missionary looked back, he saw that Lana had not fallen to the ground. Instead, a beam of dazzling starry white motes emerged from the gaping maw of Naga.

Lana swam up the stream of light, up into the atmosphere and Naga's mouth. The coils of the Sky Serpent receded into the breach in the crystal sky.

And just like the sky, Salvador Miguel's mind fractured. He and the other Spaniard witnesses collapsed where they stood, and curled into mindless babble or science and prayer. Their minds were broken forever.

Unlike the sky, which fully healed before dawn. The Indios collected the fallen bits of crystal and made jewelry and ornamental sculpture in commemoration of Lana's immortal sacrifice. They cared for Salvador Miguel and his men the best they could, but they died of thirst and starvation, unable to eat or drink in their stupor.

Joel Donato Ching Jacob is called Cupkeyk by his friends. He was the 2018 Scholastic Asian Book Award winner for 'Wing of the Locust.' He was an Editor's Choice awardee for The Best Asian Short Stories 2019 for 'Artifact from the Parent' He lives in Bay, Laguna in the Philippines with his mother and dogs. He enjoys fitness and the outdoors. Follow him on Twitter and Instagram @chimeracupkeyk.

THE CALL OF THE VOID

DAVE RING

I told everyone I would never have returned to the *Chisholm* if they hadn't made it a condition of my "probation." But I know that's not the only reason why I'm on the *Mulhall* heading back during the next Mars Approach, 26 months later after they rescued me. The security detail had me on a short leash, though it wasn't the worst cabin to be stuck in for five months. I'd already been in *that* cabin. I'd almost put it behind me, before this trip. The nightmares came back as soon as I had to sleep in no-g. But I had to admit, even though the *Chisholm* was the maker of my worst memories, it was also where my best ones came from.

"They say you just snapped."

The words startled a breath out of me that I hadn't realized I'd been holding. I didn't need to turn. Couldn't mistake Sergeant Ngyuen's raspy voice for anyone else. The most handsome and irritating member of my security detail, I was almost surprised that she had left me alone at all.

A little more than two years ago, I had finally mastered station gravity on the *Chisholm*, but sessions with Wilson still made me want to throw up. The only thing stopping me was whatever vestige of pride hadn't been eroded in the course of duty. Never again, I'll tell anyone who'll listen. I used to say I could handle anyone except child molesters. But compared to some of these jokers, those jobs were a piece of piss.

Wilson had been taciturn for the first few sessions, just like the rest of his team, until he realized that for an hour he could basically run at the mouth with whatever filth was percolating in that sorry excuse for a brain he has. Since then, he's given me material for more than a few grotesque nightmares. He seemed to think he'd had it hard growing up, but so far the worst thing he disclosed was a light thrashing from his mother when his negligence brought about the death of the family cat. He got his fifty minutes just like everyone else, so when he showed up I nodded, validated and asked gentle questions exactly like I'm supposed to. Not that he noticed. If he wasn't the CO, I might have been able to do something about him, but the only one above him was Head Officer Lusk and they were best buds. So, I dealt with it.

On the day things got twisted, I saw Irving and Singh. Those two thought therapy was hippie bullshit, so we called it career counseling and did just fine. I passed an easy hour with Irving, got a little bit into some difficult family dynamics at home. I couldn't figure out how he was so friendly with Wilson. I felt bad for him; his demanding military parents were a far sight worse than mine. Singh was even more low impact—mostly vague chatter and noncommittal observations about micro-aggressions. After Singh's session ended came the subtle-yet-irritating blip indicating that it was lunchtime.

I slung my gym bag over my shoulder, told the aeai to lock up, and headed for the main orbital. *Chisholm* station was fashioned in a bola design called an MNA3, but was colloquially referred to as Anemone. It stuck because it went with how the station looked from the outside: a central rotating orbital with about a dozen pods, each with their own micro-rotation gravity, tethered to the main orbital by flexible corridors about a good hundred meters in length. My office took up half a pod, and since my counterpart never got the appropriate documentation sorted out, it was at times an oasis of privacy.

Solitude was still priceless in space. Having the *Mulhall's* tiny o-deck to myself now, at least until Ngyuen had shown up, felt like a gift. It was strange seeing the *Chisholm* from the outside, derelict and grey against the darkness of space. None of the pods still rotated, so the MNA3 just hung in space like trash on the surface of a foetid pond, the red eye of Mars looming in the background. The *Mulhall's* trajectory had brought us into Mars' shadow, and as I watched, both the *Mulhall* and the *Chisholm* swung around the red planet and into sunlight.

I squinted at the ship's silhouette but couldn't see the pods clearly. If I was wrong, the rest of this journey would go a lot less smoothly than the beginning.

My breath caught again when I saw them in the light. I knew which pod was mine right away. It was the only one that didn't have a glistening orange filament protruding from it.

"Yeah," I said, finally. "They say a lot of things."

Singh was still stuck in the threshold chamber between my pod and the corridor when I got there. We called it the revolving door. Because the pods have their own rotation, getting into the corridor means waiting for doors to line up right. Since they don't want moving from point A to point B to require a whole lot of careful timing (or any fun really), the *Chisholm* aeai handles the timing for you. In practice, it just meant that getting between them took forever. Plenty of folks minimized moving about the orbital because the revolving doors were so obnoxious. But since they put my office, my bunk and the gym in three different pods, I'd basically memorized the timing of all the doors. I thought of them as bus schedules.

Regulation said to use the handrails, but folks usually just Supermanned down the corridor when they were by themselves. The bend took finesse, but—with practice—you learned where to put in a well-timed push so that you made it all the way to the next set of revolving doors. No idea why they hadn't put in automated hall monitor messages to chide folks for doing it yet, but I wouldn't be the one to complain about it. This time, the neon ticker told us that we'd only have to wait twenty seconds before the doors would spit us into the corridor, which was good. The problem with being the only shrink on a station was that no one ever relaxed around you. In the weightlessness of the corridor, I felt Singh eyeing me. To get it over with, I asked, "Do you mind if I rush a bit?"

Singh nodded a little too fast and I suppressed the eye roll.

"Great." I pushed off the wall as soon as I'd secured my gym bag.

I didn't notice that he'd pushed off close after me until I heard him speak from just a few yards away. "You work out a lot, Diaz?"

I startled and almost missed the extra push at the bend. It was a stupid question. Everyone knew I worked out a lot. It gave me an easy excuse for why I didn't sit with them at lunch. "I go to the gym most days, lift a bit and use the swimmer. You?"

I came to an easy stop just before the doors by trailing a hand along the ceiling and holding firmly onto the emergency track lighting, then moved carefully to the side so that Singh wouldn't crash into me. He slowed himself well enough. "I never had the patience for it. I used to like running, but can't stand having a go on a treadmill. And I never learned to swim any way but the doggy-paddle." He made a small laugh.

I shrugged. "Well, there's a few strokes that aren't too bad to learn. You could stream a couple tutorials off the sharedrive." The hell with it. "Or I could show you sometime, I suppose. Like I said, I'm there most days."

In sessions, he would look carefully to the side of my head, but here, he made eye contact. "I'll think about it, Diaz. Probably have to get over the usual lack of motivation too, but it wouldn't hurt me to exercise a bit." He patted his belly self-deprecatingly. "See you around."

That actually felt like a normal conversation for a second.

"What did Singh say? While you flayed him into strips?" Ngyuen poured herself a whiskey at the bar.

I sidled over, because I knew she'd be joining me at the *Mulhall*'s measly o-deck. I didn't say anything when her body pressed against mine from shoulder to thigh. It grounded me, a little. Made me stop wondering what it'd be like to take a long, cold fall into nothing. "What do you think?"

"C'mon, tell me."

I snorted, looked at Ngyuen's lapel cam. Irritation was making it easier to ignore the warmth she stirred in me. "You act like I don't care that you're recording me."

Ngyuen shrugged and covered the pin with her gloved hand. "You told everyone you didn't do it. If that's true, what's the big deal?"

"Singh's the big deal," I said, closing my eyes. "He didn't deserve any of this."

"But the others did. You admit that?"

I sighed. I shouldn't have said anything. But something made me want to take a risk with Ngyuen. To see if she was someone I could trust. To see if I could trust anyone. "You want to really know what happened that day?"

No one else spoke to me on my way to the gym pod aside from a brief, "Diaz," and a nod of the head. We had enough gravity on station that the gym isn't a required activity, but anyone accustomed to zero g had a hard time getting out of the habit. I changed and got into my routine: dumbbells, body weight lifts, some light stretching for my screwed up knee and then into the swimmer. Before I got injured I'd been a bit of a treadmill junkie. These days I'm not sure whether I miss the military career or the long runs more. Swimming keeps me fit, but doesn't seem to pump out as many endorphins.

Halfway through my swim, klaxons went off. I'm pretty sure they didn't put the klaxons through focus groups like they did the lunch bell, but they were terrible nonetheless. The track lighting wasn't flashing, which meant that non-emergency personnel didn't need to report anywhere, but since I was nosey, I cleaned up and went to the o-deck anyway.

I wasn't the only one who got curious. The designated gathering point was on the observation deck, where four others from the non-emergency crew had gathered. I think the only one missing was Ogunleye, the mechanic, but she was hardly one for excitability. The doc had taken my preferred chair at the back. Singh and the other two junior scientists were huddled at the railing that bifurcated the room. I found the *Chisholm*'s o-deck deeply disorienting. On the other side of the railing, five thousand square feet looking out at the universe. The view's constant movement due to the orbital rotation was one thing, but I've always had these brief and furtive compulsions to throw myself at it, to free-fall into the great expanse of space. *L'appel du vide*, my French ex-wife called it. I'd never do it, of course. The thoughts were disturbing enough that I normally avoided the o-deck as much as possible.

Today I took up a spot next to the cluster of scientists, just to see what the commotion was about. It was hard for my brain to process anything out there in that vista of whirling stars, but a space bus was being embraced by the loading dock at the edge of the viewing area, even though we weren't due to have the next batch of Martian R&R folks for another month.

"Where'd the bus come from?" the doc asked.

"The *Vigliante*. Another mining vessel," someone answered.

Once we knew it was a bus, the wait to find out why was horrifically boring. You know how that goes. I didn't have a client and never missed a chance to postpone doing up charts, so I stuck around to watch.

Irving showed up on the deck and came right up to me. "Wilson needs you downstairs, Diaz."

"Really?" I followed him without waiting for a pointless reply.

Downstairs wasn't really accurate, but we used the term for the half of the station dedicated to docking, storage and maintenance. Irving brought me to the cargo hold. The other three soldiers were there, plus Wilson, Head Officer Lusk and presumably the two former occupants of the shuttle. Too many people for the size of the room. Two privates stood there shiftily, their hands twitching towards absent weapons. The sergeant looked mean, as usual, her truncheon held ready and her eyes fixed on the two strangers.

A thin cot had been set up for a white man with a shiny, bald head. He currently lay motionless but for the slight rise and fall of his chest. He wore dusty work clothes. Next to him, cross-legged on the floor and hands behind her head, sat a stocky woman, her hair wrapped up in a kerchief. Her fatigues were spotted with grease and a fuzzy orange mold.

"Diaz is here, sir," Irving announced. The woman took a look at me. Her face was puffy, her eyes stained red. I nodded to her. She didn't respond.

"These two are your purview, Diaz." Something about the tone of Wilson's voice reminded me of a child poking at some poor thing with a stick. "Tell her, Rodriguez."

"You the shrink?" the woman asked, lips pursed. "Have I got a livewire for you, then."

Five or six questions jostled for position on my tongue. The woman jerked her chin in the direction of her prone companion. "He's doped up at the moment but he's got space rage and a bad sense of humour. And he's the reason the rest of the *Vigliante*'s team is taking a nap out in vacuum."

"I see," I said. My heart sped up. I hadn't had a single case like this in my entire posting so far. The recommended protocol for situational explosive disorder—space rage—was cell maintenance and then shipping back to Earth. This would be the first I'd ever treated and also the first for the Mars orbital. I was confident in my skills of assessment, but I didn't relish the idea of forging a new policy.

"You were thinking about policy, just then? Not the fact that he'd killed people?" Ngyuen's eyebrow broadcast her skepticism.

She was trying to goad me, but I was past that. "It hadn't sunk in yet. And you know what it's like. Accidents happen. People come up with all sorts of reasons for why." We'd entered comms range of the *Chisholm*. I stepped away from the window and skimmed the console feeds by the wall. They were receiving data packets. I didn't push my luck by trying to scan the contents, but I let my hopes get up.

"You didn't believe it, even then," Ngyuen guessed as I returned to her side.

"Space rage is a pop diagnosis. Like DID used to be."

"Like what?"

"Sorry. Dissociative identity disorder."

"I'm still not—"

My probation officer certainly wasn't a psychology major. "Sorry. Multiple personalities."

Ngyuen shook it off. "The military has an acronym or two, you know."

"Right." I snorted. If she had been a psychology major, she might have clocked that I was a former officer.

"So what, you tell Wilson where to stick it?"

"I wish," I said.

The supposed space rager was named Private Gary Johnson.

They set up his cell in the other half of the pod my office was in. Wilson gave me a set of cuffs that could be activated and deactivated remotely. Gary would lock himself to the bed we'd moved in there, which had been riveted to the floor, and then I would unlock his door and take a seat on the armchair. I'd been told not to get close enough to him that he could touch me, but I'd ignored it a couple times. Once to hand him a drink and another time to look at something on his reader.

I liked Gary. His sessions were easy. He had warm affect and a kind understanding of the role I had to play in the whole affair. He wasn't telling me everything, no, but then no client ever really told their therapist everything. We had a good therapeutic rapport. I spent a lot of time talking to him and trying to hammer out a solid diagnosis, but it just wasn't there.

"Gary, I know it's hard, but I need you to tell me about the day that it happened."

His eyes welled up with tears. It could have been theater, yes, but it didn't scan that way. "It was just like every other day, I swear. I wasn't losing it. And I didn't even do it by accident. I don't even know how I'd vent the airlocks on purpose, let alone by losing my shit and hitting the wrong buttons."

"It sounds like you were pretty upset by what happened. And the idea that you were involved."

"That's the fricking understatement of the century." He threw himself back in his chair, shaking his shackled leg fruitlessly.

"Sorry, Gary," I said. "I'm not trying to be provocative. I'm just trying not to put words in your mouth."

"You know," he said, looking over my shoulder. "You're not supposed to get involved with other folks on a long gig. Tight quarters, don't shit where you eat, that sort of thing. But me and Dawson, I think there was something there maybe. And now he's a fricking ice cube stuck to the hull of our ship."

I didn't have to say anything in response, not really, but I felt like my heart spasmed, he sounded so forlorn. "It's one of the most unpleasant truths in the galaxy, Gary, that being open to love can bring us both the greatest joys and greatest pains of our lives."

We didn't talk for awhile after that, just sat in silence, sharing space together.

"You're a bit of a fortune cookie dispenser, aren't you?" Ngyuen asked, laughing a bit.

I stared her down. She fidgeted with her short curls before returning her hand to cover the lapel cam.

"Sorry, I didn't mean anything by it."

I thought about stopping, but it was too hard to care. I kept one eye on the anklet that told the *Mulhall*'s aeai where I was at all times. Its tiny red eye blinked steadily. I was only half telling the story for Ngyuen. I also wanted to tell it for Singh.

Lieutenant Ileana Rodriguez spoke her own name with an ugliness that I found fascinating, giving the first "a" an awful nasal emphasis. She sought me out a number of times each day.

"You wouldn't believe what he was like when I found him," she'd say. "You should send him back immediately." Rodriguez didn't seem to understand that it would be weeks before a bus showed up to remove him. We only made the trip from Earth every two years, after all. She moved with a jerky awkwardness that made me question her military record. I couldn't imagine her being the sharpshooter it claimed she was.

Rodriguez would tell me symptoms that Gary had been demonstrating back on Mars. Each one exactly like the manual, nothing like the patient I was working with.

Days of this. I would run through the scenario with Gary, picking out details for my reports, and Rodriguez would show up like a cardboard cutout of a witness, trying to peer at my notes while feeding me tidbits.

She was the obvious suspect, of course. But she knew that, and she'd brought the black box from their ship as her alibi. The official feed from the black box showed her coordinates to be in her bunk asleep during the incident, well away from any controls, as well as the airlocks in question. Rodriguez had an extensive engineering resume, so I had no doubt she could have tampered with the feed, but there was nothing I could do for now but make sure that all of our interactions were recorded.

The night before I gave my recommendation, I barely slept. When I recommended to Lusk that Gary be released, Rodriguez was furious. Wilson didn't like it either. He swore up and down, told me that he'd already gotten all the clearance from Earth to get Gary shipped back, even though I hadn't given him the go ahead. He called me some names too. And, even though I felt my cheeks burning with embarrassment, I stuck to my guns and refused to change it.

Gary got released from my extended office, put in a regular cabin, still locked but now let out occasionally under military supervision instead of twice daily therapy.

The day after that Wilson found Gary bleeding out in the dining hall. He'd scooped out most of his own insides after stabbing Irving through the eye with a fork.

"Huh," Ngyuen said. "All the reports said Singh died first. When Gary infected you with space rage."

"Reports? You liar. The only place you read that was in a tabloid."

Ngyuen looked away. "I knew I'd be escorting you, didn't I? They wouldn't tell me anything. My briefing was two paragraphs long.

Couldn't be totally unprepared."

"Yeah." My tongue was acid. "Be a shame for you to be an unbiased security detail. Wouldn't want that."

"The *Mulhall*'s specs don't make sense, either. Not for a simple escort. And there are three cargo bays that don't show up on my reports. I wonder if you know anything about that."

I raised my eyebrows. "So that's what you've been doing when you're not badgering me."

Ngyuen turned a knob on her label cam, lowered her glove and rested it on my arm.

"What are you doing?" I asked, despite knowing full well.

"So I'm a terrible person. You'd still sleep with me though, wouldn't you?"

I blinked. "I—" Was I blushing?

"It's okay," Ngyuen said, grinning. "I just wanted you to be sure I turned the camera off."

I pulled back a little, but didn't brush off her arm. I didn't want to come across too much the ingénue. But if something didn't go right with Plan A, having my probation officer in my palm wouldn't hurt. "Oh. So you don't —"

"Oh, I do. I would. You show up in my bunk anytime, it's on, I promise. But, that's hardly professional of me." She squeezed my forearm.

It had been a long time since someone had made an overture towards me. Considering my reputation. I felt a little off balance until I looked down at the anklet. While I watched, the blinking red light changed to green, and then stopped. An anxiety I had been ignoring faded. "I'm flattered, I just—"

"C'mon, tell me the rest," Ngyuen said. "I know I have it all wrong. There were no aliens, no jealous lovers. What really happened?"

Right back to that. I snorted again, annoyed at myself. Screw it. She'll find out soon enough. "Well, my theory is that there *were* aliens."

Somehow, the computer had my credentials as the only crew in the dining room on file, even though the cam footage was down for that hour and everyone knew I had no idea how to do that kind of wizardry. Wilson came after me as soon as he could. He found me in the gym, solo, dragged me out of the swimmer. He got in two good ones, my belly and the temple, before I broke his nose.

I legged it, water flying off me into no-g as soon as I left the gym. Only thing that got me to my office in one piece was my mental bus schedule—Wilson went slamming into the glass when he came for me.

Lusk should have reprimanded Wilson, but he didn't. There should have been a trial too, however our approach to the work site had been completed, and now all the miners were required to work doubles. Rodriguez complained about it to anyone who would listen, but Lusk's priority was the worksite. The surveyors even found an unexpected source of helium, which meant bonuses for everyone. The o-deck view became polluted with bustling tankers.

Instead of legal proceedings, Lusk put us all on high alert. No traveling anywhere without a buddy. Singh was assigned to me. I hated it until I realized that if I didn't go anywhere until Singh got me, Wilson wouldn't try to break my head again. Singh wasn't completely willing to give up lunch, not when half the crew thought I was the one that killed Gary. Every third day, we'd go to the gym. He was self-conscious in his swimming togs, which surprised me. Most folks don't get too far in the military with their modesty intact. Singh really was a terrible swimmer, all thrashing limbs and lolling tongue at first. But he was a good listener, eager to improve his form, and soon his breast stroke was more precise than mine. He talked about his life, his two girls. His ex-wife. Asked me about mine, then didn't mind when I couldn't shut up about how we should never have gotten together.

We got closer than we should have. Fraternized, I mean. Just once, after a good workout, both of us rank and sore. I'd never been with a man before. I hadn't realized what it would feel like; there was just so much hair everywhere. It wasn't bad in and of itself, just not what I was used to. Singh wasn't used to letting someone else be in control, so we never got into a good rhythm. As soon as it was over, we shared a look and started cracking up. Saved it from being awkward. Never again, I decided.

Lunches could have been worse, I'll give him that. With Singh there, folks weren't as rude as they could have been. I don't think people realized how sarcastic I was being before. They just thought I was rude. It felt strange, but a couple weeks of high alert brought me closer to the crew than I'd ever been before. Normally after a casualty, everyone would have been required to have mandatory sessions with me, but because I was one of the suspects, they relaxed that regulation. It was strange to think that being considered a possible murderer had improved my social standing, but it was what happened. Plus, no one had liked Wilson but Irving, so it didn't hurt my rep when folks figured out it was me who'd rearranged his face.

Lusk finally got around to something approaching a trial a few weeks later, after the worksite had been exhausted. And when they wheeled Gary out of the impromptu mortuary, well. I've seen the footage. His skin had been worn thin as paper, a diaphanous sheath for the spores inside. Lusk's finger, gently prodding Gary's cheek, led to the body bursting like an awful piñata.

Lusk and a few soldiers all got mouthfuls. They couldn't avoid it.

Hours later, someone found Rodriguez bleeding out in her bunk. She'd murdered her bunkmate with a torn off attachment from the wash-unit.

It only took a day for her skin to decompose. The crew wasn't stupid. They knew that Lusk was a carrier. Mutiny wasn't far behind. Not that it did anything for them.

Ngyuen exhaled, her breath ragged. I'd thought confessing the liaison with Singh might get a rise out of her, but it was short-lived. Sometime during my description of the fungal spores, she'd withdrawn her arm. "The spores were—?"

"Controlling her? Yeah, that's my best bet. Something like that. That's why I'm not ruling out aliens."

Ngyuen rolled her eyes and then swore when she saw I was serious, staring out the window at the lurid filaments protruding from the Chisholm's pods. "And you avoided death by..."

"Singh saved me. When Lusk and Wilson died, he was the highest-ranking soldier left. He worked with Ogunleye to shut off the aeai connecting the pods to the station."

"He didn't come with you?" Ngyuen asked, quietly. She knew what was coming.

"He was already a goner. And someone needed to live."

She nodded, pounded her fist against my back in sympathy. Her hand lingered afterward, smoothing down the shoulder of my travel gear and lingering on the small of my back.

"They all did awful things, when they got infected," I said, wishing I still didn't see flashes of it. Ogunleye finally succumbed, torturing Singh while he was still alive. He made me promise to stay with him on the comm until the end. His screams had etched themselves into my dreams. What kind of person can live for months on a space station full of dead bodies? "Except for Rodriguez. Everyone else lost their minds, was consumed by violence.

They couldn't help it. Rodriguez though, she was different. She was the carrier."

Ngyuen tapped the fake glass that showed us the *Chisholm*'s wreckage. "We're not here for you to see this, are we?"

"No," I said, shaking my head. "This is just a pitstop. We're here to see what's left of the *Vigliante*."

Ngyuen whistled. "I got it all wrong. So why are you telling me, huh? This must all be classified." Her hand inched lower, just shy of the curve of my ass.

"Check your mission brief. It should have been updated recently." Ngyuen went to the console. I tried not to smirk when her eyes widened. My field promotion had finally gone through.

"I— ma'am, I'm so sorry for my presumption. Captain, I mean." Ngyuen's cheeks were burning and she stared at the floor, hand snapping up in a sharp salute.

I laughed, but kindly I hoped. "At ease, soldier."

Ngyuen's eyes lifted up slowly, until she once again met my gaze. "Please accept my sincere apologies, Captain. I spoke unbefitting to a member of your crew. It was inappropriate for me to interrogate you."

"You could hardly have known. Hell, I didn't know for sure."

"Captain, I—"

I waved her off, turning away from the window, and pointed to the Mulhall's console. The *Vigliante*'s blueprint jumped onto the screen beside it, rotating slowly. "Apology accepted, Ngyuen. I told you for a reason."

Now she looked embarrassed *and* intrigued. "Captain, forgive me. What's the reason?"

"What do you think, soldier?" I was hardly going to tell her I wanted to know if I was still capable of friendship after watching my whole crew murder each other before my eyes. My fingernail slid along her jaw, making her look me in the eye. "You're the one who'll be leading the squadron going to *Vigliante* with me."

Ngyuen swallowed, nervous as hell. "Yes, ma'am."

"Consider it a mission briefing." A little spark of sadism flared in me. Was this what I had instead? "Did you still want me to come by your bunk later?"

"Oh, shit. Ma'am—Captain—" Ngyuen's swagger was gone. Now the rasp just annoyed me.

"You're dismissed, soldier." I tried to stave off my irritation when relief flashed across Ngyuen's face.

I poured myself a tumbler of whiskey before returning to the projection of the *Chisholm* on the o-deck screen. The liquor's burn tethered me, kept my stomach from somersaulting into the darkness. I leaned into the slight wantonness of it. I laughed. I wasn't broken, even though I had every right to be. There'd be time enough for second chances and following new orders. For now, I just wanted to look out the window and prove to myself that I wouldn't jump.

"For Singh," I said aloud. And I think I also meant, maybe for the first time, *for me.*

dave ring is the chair of the OutWrite LGBTQ Book Festival in Washington, DC. He has stories featured or forthcoming in a number of publications, including *Fireside Fiction*, *GlitterShip*, and *A Punk Rock Future*. He is the publisher and managing editor of Neon Hemlock Press, as well as the editor of *Broken Metropolis: Queer Tales of a City That Never Was* from Mason Jar Press. More info at www.dave-ring.com. Follow him at @slickhop.

Everything Old Is New Again

Willow Croft

The vintage Harley rumbled down the quiet suburban street. He imagined them in there, their flimsy beds they bought from IKEA vibrating them awake with the loud growl from his bike. Disturbing their sad twenty-first-century take on suburban conformity with their open floor plans and stainless-steel appliances that reminded him more of the kitchens he'd worked in as a kid. These new suburbanites were far from hip, and not far enough from the fifties for his own comfort. Earl still resented it; the gentrification that had taken over the neighbourhood he'd grown up in.

He'd moved into his mother's house after she passed away, but he never talked to any of the young couples that lived in the concrete monstrosities that replaced cozy houses like his mother's. He just scowled at them, cracking his knuckles and flexing his muscles underneath his leather jacket. Finally, they seemed to get the hint, and stopped inviting them to their vegan, non-GMO potlucks. *Whatever the hell GMO was, anyway.* Something to do with that stupid butterfly that was now appearing on everything from mustard to soda. He wished he'd been the one to come up with that marketing scam—they had to be rich by now. But he had enough money from his momma's estate for anything he wanted, including plenty of beer at the biker bar that had managed to survive the downtown's takeover by trendy coffee shops.

And he and his friends were survivors, too. Not just of the war, but of the old age that was creeping up on them. Just last month, Juan had died. Slipped and fell in his shower, his son said when he called them. Juan's son had asked the gang to go over and clean out the house, host a sale, and donate the proceeds to a local veterans' charity.

Earl sighed and turned off the engine, limping a little as he climbed the steps to his front door. He didn't even feel that old, just a little twinge in his knees right before a rain. He stuck the key in but the lock wouldn't turn. He yanked the key out and squinted at it. Juan's key, not his. Probably should take it off. But he wanted to keep it close, as if he could head over to Juan's old house, and roust him for an evening of biker-style troublemaking that they'd done as kids. Before Earl, himself, had got arrested and sent to juvie prison, for crimes the world would never know about. For crimes he didn't even want to know about. Crimes fueled by rage he also tried to forget.

His scarred hands shook a little as he shoved his own key in the lock. He felt the tightness in his chest ease as the lock turned. The door screeched a complaint as he opened it and stepped inside. *Safe as houses,* as his momma used to say. He'd never been one to play it safe, but that was before they came. Before the visitors arrived. He'd told Darius, once, about his dreams. Figured his biker buddy would know, being an occultist and all. But he just stared at him over his pint.

"Dreams are just dreams," he'd said, shifting his gaze past Earl and towards the dartboard on the wall.

Probably didn't even remember, if he ever did know. Not too long after that, Darius's daughter had him checked into an assisted living facility when his dementia got too bad for him to live on his own. And Earl's dreams continued. With each night, they got more vivid. More real. It took him even longer to realize where he was after the dreams. Sometimes he didn't even recognize the flowered wallpaper on the walls. All he could see were the creatures. Coming at him with too many arms and legs and eyes. Dark, piercing eyes that jabbed straight into his mind, into his soul, and dug out all his secrets. The ones not even his biker buddies knew about.

He switched on the hall light, and locked the door behind him; locked all three locks and slid the chain. He hung his leather jacket on the wrought iron coatrack by the door. He hadn't even replaced his mother's antique furniture. It gave him comfort in the same way Earl's key had. It was familiar and known, against the strange world that his dreams drug him into night after night. He unlaced his boots, placing them side by side on the mat. He padded down the hall, the old wood floor rough and prickly underneath his feet.

And he was afraid. Afraid that if he changed anything, the spirits would be unhappy. That the creatures from his dreams would spill out into reality. Out into his safe haven. He flicked the switch in the bedroom. The room where most of the spirits lived. The two stained-glass lamps that flanked the four-poster bed illuminated the eyes of the spirits. The first one had come from Darius, only he didn't realize what a powerful force lay behind those glassy eyes. It had ended up on the shelf in his bedroom.

Lots of bikers had stuffed bears strapped to their motorcycle seats, but he'd felt silly with it riding along behind him. He was a grown man, not a child.

But the bear became a comfort to him. Its warm amber-glass eyes were nothing like the soulless eyes of the creatures in his dreams. The eyes only reflected what was in the room, not the horrors of a million evils. And so began his collection. Not new stuffed toys; old ones that had lived. Old ones that had been through wars just like he had, with bare fur patches and missing eyes. But if one sparkling glass remained, that was good enough. His shelf filled with the stuffed animals he'd bought at garage sales. His guardians that watched over him as he slept, and dreamed.

"Coming," the creatures would whisper in their raspy voices. "Coming for you. Coming for all of you."

He knew they couldn't reach him, not since he'd amassed his toy army, but he still shrank back. The creatures crawled and slithered and oozed towards him, spilling out of their sleek ship. Until they smacked into the glass wall that had appeared the first night he'd put the bear on his shelf. Tentacles smacked against the glass, leaving behind long trails of dripping slime. He shivered in his sleep. But it was better than the slime left behind as the creatures pulled out his entrails and carried them back to their ship, dragging his still-living corpse behind them. Those same long fingernails scrabbled on the glass. A glass wall that moved the creatures further away from him with each new stuffed animal he bought and shelved.

Gotta remember to lube up the door hinges, he thought, as he turned over in his sleep. But he didn't remember this morning, either. Only remembered the creatures and their strange ship, with the swirling colors that, in turn, reminded him of his mother's opal wedding ring. It still took him a long time to remember where he was, though. But at least he was now sleeping through the night. He'd even been able to pick up a few shifts at the service garage he used to work at.

On this morning, like every other morning, the room faded back into his view. Sunlight fell across him in ribbons from the blinds at the window. He heard yelling as the young couple from next door herded their kids into the battery-powered vehicle they used to transport their kids to one of the million activities they forced on those poor kids. It was Saturday, so it was probably some sort of sports event. He scanned the room one more time. No monsters. The toys winked at him as he got out of bed. Somewhere along the way, they'd become more than guardians. They'd become friends, taking the edge of the loneliness of the self that he couldn't change.

The one that had never married. Never even wanted to marry, after the war scarred him in ways not even his childhood had. And never wanted to have kids, in case he would make them live in the same sort of hell he'd grown up in. Until the day he'd killed the demons that populated that hell. He'd almost gotten away with it, too, were it not for his brother. Who hadn't lived very long after he testified in court. He looked at the clock. Almost nine.

Time to get to work. He crawled out of bed, his head aching from the alcohol the night before. He dressed in his work clothes and boots and headed outside. One of the young men from next door was watering his front-yard vegetable garden. Earl kicked his motorcycle to life and backed it out of the driveway. Earl gave it more gas when he straightened out and the bike rumbled even louder. The young man glared at him. Earl greeted him right back, extending his middle finger up as he sped past. He was almost to the shop when a bright neon green sign caught his eye.

"Yard Sale," it blazed. The hand-drawn arrow pointed right.

He slid the bike neatly around the turn and pulled up in front of another one of those property-line-to-property-line featureless concrete homes. It was nearing closer to ten, and most of the tables looked like they had been picked over. If there had been stuffed animals, they were already gone. Except for one; a blue-and-white toy shoved between two plastic flamingo tumblers. He closed his eyes. Tentacles slid towards him. He felt his chest tighten.

"Can I help you?"

He opened his eyes. A young man stood there, wearing what looked like a ski cap despite the warmth of the morning.

"I'll, uh, take this little guy." He pointed to the stuffed octopus.

The young man stared at him, then shrugged. "Fifty cents."

"It's for my daughter," he said, digging into his pocket and handing over the coins.

"I didn't ask," the young man responded in that snotty, entitled tone all the kids had today. The young man pocketed the coins and went back to texting on his phone.

Earl's fist clenched around the little octopus. *No. Don't do it. Get to work. Work, and then the bar, to take the edge off.* He spun around and stomped off to his bike, shoving the octopus in the saddlebag before he hopped on. He kicked the motorcycle to life and rumbled off to the shop. He didn't calm down until he was halfway through repairs on an old Jaguar. Envisioning that each twist of the screw was a tighter squeeze around that young man's neck helped. As did his first cold beer after his shift. Or, actually the tenth cold beer as he sat on his stool in the dark bar. *Safe as houses.* He drank until the bartender cut him off. *The first time in years,* he thought, wobbling back and forth on his stool. He'd been buying rounds and his biker buddies were too drunk themselves as wobbled all the way off his stool and stumbled out to his bike. The world, too, was wobbling. It righted itself miraculously when he swung his leg over the seat and started it up.

He was too drunk to let it rumble in the carport long enough to annoy his neighbours. *The octopus, don't forget the octopus.* He burped and almost puked as he fumbled in the saddlebag for the toy. He made it off the bike and up the stairs without falling.

At least not all the way. He laughed but that made the world wobble again so he quit. Somehow he managed to get the right key into the right door lock on his first try. He didn't dare take his boots off, not unless he wanted to sleep it off in the hall, and he held onto the wall as he lurched down to his bedroom. He flopped, belly up, on the bed, the stuffed octopus still clutched in his hand.

He slept, and did not dream. He didn't have to. The four-poster bed began to shake. One by one the stuffed animals—his guardians—fell off the shelf. He slept on, his snores keeping time with the rumbling underneath him. Bright blue light replaced the dim amber glow of the streetlight outside the window.

He slept on, and did not hear them coming. Did not hear the squelching, scrabbling, slithering noises as the creatures crawled down the hall. He did not hear as they rose to full height over him with a series of creaking, crackling sounds. He did not feel it as one of the creatures plucked the tiny octopus from his hand and tucked it under one of its many arms. He did not hear as the creature murmured to the stuffed octopus in a strange language. But he heard it when all the creatures boomed at once.

"We are here."

And they stooped down to his level. And Earl's fists; his violent, rage-driven, ageing fists were useless against them. Against the invasion which had just begun.

Willow Croft currently lives in the high desert, but dreams of a home by a tumultuous ocean. When she's not writing, she's caring for her rescued calico, Moon Pie.

Her work has appeared in *Rock N' Roll Horror Zine*, *Mad Scientist Journal*, *Speculative 66*, and *Neon Druid: An Anthology of Urban Celtic Fantasy*.

Find our more here: willowcroft.blog or on Twitter: WillowCroft16.

EDGING TOWARD OBLIVION

RYAN PRIEST

Those first few days felt like the beginnings of another great let down, another catastrophe averted. Fear and Imagination gave way to sterile and blasé explanations by slow speaking experts on TV. Why couldn't they ever just let something magical be magical? The Earth had suddenly gained a new moon in the sky; let people be amazed.

After three days everyone was used to it. McDonalds' had already compiled a commercial about how the Double Moon was an excuse to eat more French fries. Conspiracy nuts said it was the end of the world. Men and women with degrees in the subject said it was an optical illusion, the atmosphere, solar winds etc. There was no way a new and unknown moon could have arrived overnight.

"It was hiding around the other side of the Sun." Robbie said staring up at the bright blue sky out of the office window. In the day, the Double Moon was as invisible as the normal Moon. Robbie was director of the New Technology division. This meant that he was Milt's supervisor and as such, free to walk up to his desk anytime he wanted to chitchat.

"How could an object the size of the Moon have been hiding, even behind the Sun, and simply gone unnoticed for the last six thousand years of human history?" Milton was annoyed that he'd been interrupted. He was trying to program a new feature for the company's app. It took a lot of concentration whereas Robbie's job seemed to consist of bouncing from desk to desk, office to office, accomplishing absolutely nothing. Today Robbie was going on about the Double Moon. Explaining the theory he'd just read on the internet.

"It *hasn't* gone unnoticed. Several translators have said ancient astronomers were aware of a sister planet to Earth. Today's astronomers call them crackpots but here it is."

"Robbie, I have a lot of work to do."

"Milton, stop for a second and consider. What if there was another planet rotating around the Sun... vertically?" Robbie was very pleased with himself for presenting this possibility.

Software engineers are still engineers so Milton thought about it for a second. He built a model of the solar system in his mind's eye. He watched the Earth spinning around and then imagined, rather than spinning on a horizontal, elliptical plane, this new planet rotated pole to pole of the Sun. "Well, there's a chance we wouldn't notice for a while. If those orbits were arranged in just such a way that we routinely avoided each other."

"See!?" Robbie smiled widely.

"So, we're going to smash into this new planet and all die?"

"Probably! Unless we do something." Robbie's giddiness belied the fact he was talking about global cataclysm. Milton decided to see just how much faith he had in this new idea.

"Well, does that mean we can close the office down and go home?"

"No."

"I didn't think so. Look Robbie, I have a lot of work to do."

"Say, you ever get in touch with Candy's friend Charlotte?" Robbie changed the subject, blindsiding Milton. Robbie's wife, Candy had been trying to set Milton up with one or another of her friends for months.

"Tell her I'm not looking to get into a relationship now."

"C'mon! No one is talking about a relationship. That woman is desperate. She just wants to be shown a fun night out and then it's a sure thing."

"I'm not interested." Milton was trying to play it cool but he was probably blushing. He hated blushing because there was always some ignorant asshole who'd yell out "I didn't know black people could blush." and then it would just cause him to redden even further. He hated Robbie prying into his private life. Robbie was his boss, the face of his employer, not a human being he could ever be real with. How was he supposed to explain to Robbie that he wanted nothing to do with his wife's dull friends? How could he ever get it across that he had found something so much better?

That night on evening news they were saying that the second moon was getting bigger every night. No, a collision with a giant celestial body was not getting closer. The optical illusion was simply getting wider. The experts, astronomers pleased-as-punch to be let on television, promised it'd be gone within a week or two.

The evening news was part of Milton's daily ritual. There was no reason to it, neither spiritual nor otherwise, but he liked his set routine; it seemed to imbue everything with a certain formal gravitas.

Each day returning home from work he tried to keep everything the same. From using his left foot to walk through the door, to hanging his keys on the hook. One shoe off, then the other. He warmed dinner up at six. Ate it at six-fifteen while he watched the news, next dishes, then trash. He would then lay out clothes for the morning if they were already clean otherwise, laundry. By seven-thirty everything was done and he could begin.

Milt shot back to reality out of breath. He was sweating, confused. He looked over at the clock. Two am. He rolled off of his couch and stumbled into his bedroom. He could shower in the morning. He dropped down to his bed and fell fast asleep. The ritual complete.

"See, it's getting bigger because it's a planet and it's coming to hit us." Robbie had stopped everyone from working to discuss the Double Moon. He had been playful about it the day before but now he was serious.

Milt didn't mind. He was tired and try as he might to avoid it, his work was always total shit whenever he was fatigued.

"What if? You guy, what if?" Robbie let it hang in the air. "What would you do if this it, if this is the end of the world?"

Spend time with their families. Shoot heroin just to see what it was like. Fuck anyone who couldn't run away fast enough. Everyone had different but ultimately the same answer. They didn't *know* what they'd do. They didn't have a plan. They lived their lives from moment to moment, trying to fill some imaginary jar with experiences as an end in and of itself. But not Milton.

"I don't know, I guess I'd want to be with my family." Milton lied to be like everyone else. He lied to hide his true self. He lied because he was not like these people, he was on a different level and they'd never understand.

He lied because he knew exactly what he'd do and, because of that, he alone was unafraid of the end of the world.

"Milton, listen, you don't want to let life pass you by. Even if this isn't the end. C'mon man, give Charlotte a call." Robbie pestered.

At a certain point, it was sexual harassment. Pimping him out to his wife's friend. Some needy, boring woman, amateur in the art of pleasure. One more human bag, filled with farts and giggles yet expecting deferential pampering. Romance seemed like some voluntary servitude at the end of which, if everything went in your favor, you could be paid with awkward, teenage-like sex with another thirty-something.

That night the news admitted that there was a slight chance that it wasn't an illusion. On the internet, men and women with high powered telescopes were showing close-up videos. It didn't look like some visual illusion. It looked like a planet.

It was almost seven-thirty. Now, more than ever, Milt had to complete his ritual. He had a purpose and even a goal that was only now beginning form itself out from the shadows of his periphery. He turned up his speakers, played his song, the song that put him in the right headspace for the coming transformation.

He allowed himself to move to the music, then with it and ultimately to become it. Dancing around his apartment like some wild mystic, freeing himself of all cares while at the same time speeding up the rhythm of his heart. As Nina Simone sang those extended last notes of "Feeling Good", Milt collapsed on his couch. He flipped on the television and undid his pants.

Edging could be described as a transcendental form of tantric onanism. That is a nice way of saying that edging is perpetual masturbation, when a man brings himself to the brink of climax and then pulls back, so he can keep masturbating longer.

Pornographic images danced across the television screen illuminating the darkened room. Groans, squeaks and the slapping sound of wet skin hitting wet skin, groans, squeaks all filled the air. Transfixed and mouth-breathing Milton sat with his pants now around his ankles, stroking himself. This lasted for hours. Sub-human, half in this world and one foot in some existence that held only divine pleasure.

After so long, so much work, so much pumping, the finish always felt the same. Everything. All emotion, all pain, all pleasure, oneness. Then it was over. His mind snapped back in place, as if coming out of trance. He was messy and there was always the feeling that it had all ended too soon, if he could have held out a few more seconds then... he didn't know what but he knew it'd be wonderful.

The next day no one did any work. A good percentage of the company hadn't come in and those who had were glued to television screens. Everyone watched the panicked minute by minute coverage. Now, the experts were saying it wasn't an illusion and that they'd never said it was. They all walked back their prior statements, tried to save their reputations in a world that seemed closer and closer to the end with every passing second. Now the Double Moon was visible in the daytime, it measured at five or six inches on any ruler held up to the sky. On its best day, at the very best angle, you're lucky to get three inches out of the real Moon.

"We're all going to die!" Robbie cried into his hands. Everyone at the office was crying. Everyone except for Milt who sat furiously tapping his foot.

With a very somber voice the current expert said that this would literally be the last night on Earth.

"I don't want to die a virgin!" Ted from marketing screamed, twenty-six and already balding; but it didn't matter, he wouldn't lose any more hair.

"There's so much I never did too!" Becky from marketing cried as she ran to Ted's chair, sending them both rolling over backwards.

"No judgement, let's just *be* together. Total acceptance!" Robbie cried out. He tried and failed to tear his shirt off while he dove into the forming pile of coworkers.

But Milt was already heading towards the door. He would never see these people again and he was fine with that.

"C'mon Milt, it's the end!" Robbie yelled. "Let's go out happy!"

The door swished shut without another word, leaving the amateurs to their attempt at happiness. Milt hurried home, the new Double Moon was wide overhead, looking down hungrily on all it would soon devour.

Robbie, Becky and the others, what did they know about happiness? What did they know about life? Everyone had a different answer when asked what the meaning of life is. Long ago, Milton had answered it for himself. There was no meaning. No inherent meaning at least. No objective, same for everyone, innate in and of itself meaning. Not in the slightest. There was only pain and loss. Those were the only experiences we were all universally guaranteed to experience.

So why go on? For the fleeting moments of happiness? To populate the over-crowded Earth with more victims for its unending cruelty? To try to establish an aesthetic sense of balanced contentment like some Buddhist? To invent something new or do something great so that your name would outlive you? Several people had different solutions to the problem of pointlessness. All of those had been the wrong answer. With the end of the world sweeping ever and ever closer, no amount of great deeds would see your name remembered, no statue or tower would last. No balance would ever be achieved. All pursuits in this world had just been made irredeemably pointless.

But this world was not Milton's concern. His had been a different solution, a different way out of the melancholy brought on by realizing his personal insignificance. He had turned inward. He had analyzed life. What made it worth living? If anything, pleasure. The Dalai Llama defined happiness as the search for peace and the avoidance of suffering. But Milt knew there was another level. Every thirteen-year-old boy and most likely every girl discovers very quickly that there's a certain happiness out there greater than the mere absence of pain. If only there was a way to make that pleasure last longer than two or three seconds.

Milton got home and shut the door, not that it mattered. He disrobed completely. He didn't bother to dance, his heart was already racing and his mind was already locked in. He turned on the television, set it to his private playlist and one last time, he began.

He had always liked sex, masturbation, feeling good. It was only when he sat back and really analyzed it did he figure out what he liked about it. The change. From the time he became aroused until the time he orgasmed, he would be in a different headspace. Much like being drunk, most people didn't realize the effect until it was gone. That confusion that swept over him afterwards, the feeling like he'd just woken up, that was because he *had*. Some autonomic function, some programming in his animal brain would take over and move his body, cause his hand to stroke, fed itself on sexuality and sexual imagery. While all this happened, the volume on his higher self, his logic, his analytical reservation, would decrease, instead replaced by this glowing pleasure, this riotous and electrified hunger, this pure singularity of purpose. The climb, the perpetual climb towards ecstasy, each step closer feeling better and better.

The sun was being blotted out of the sky. Darkness fell under the shadow of the coming Double Moon. Milt kept going. For years he'd done this. For hours every night, he would play his own body like an instrument, learning to stretch out the sweet notes of pleasure for as long as possible.

Robbie had probably already come. A quick second, a tortured face and a drop of glue. Then he was just Robbie again, spent and incapable of getting back to that place. The shame, regret, pains from rough and unpracticed fingers, that's all they could expect back at work. Milt was going deep, surfing long and undulated waves of pleasure, edging him closer and closer towards the end but then he'd stop, pull back, breathe.

His heart was still beating, his adrenalized hormones rampaging through his veins, his mind somewhere else and he'd start up again, put his foot back on the pedal and he's continue. Outside there were car alarms going off, the wind has become violent and there was so much screaming. Long wails from human beings with no place left to go, lives unfulfilled and wasted.

By his accounting, Milt had spent a far greater percentage of his life feeling absolute pleasure than most people. Only hardcore heroin junkies could match edgers in their capacity to simply live inside of pleasure. Only now, with trees uprooting and taking flight and oceans overflowing with city-crushing tidal waves, was it clear that junkies and chromic masturbators had been on the right track. Every sweaty mile run by a fitness freak, every continued learning class taken by bookish nerd, every dollar earned by some greedy billionaire, was all for nothing. Not only had they wasted so many hours that could have been given over to pleasure, but now in these final minutes they didn't even know how to turn on that faucet of bliss.

Volcanoes spewed forth lava blood from Earth's churning insides as she and this new Double Moon both pulled towards one another with the force of their combined gravity. The ground cracked and split, fissures belched forth steam and other long buried gasses. Milt continued pumping away, ogling the screen as people who were probably now dying, performed wild and unbridled acts with perfect bodies. The power finally went out with a loud pop and a snap. All the beautiful, sexual people had now blinked forever out of existence too.

Milton's apartment shook and the walls began to crack and crumble. He closed his eyes and continued, willing forth images, scenarios, sounds and scents that his body hungered for. He worked himself harder, faster, he was all in, willing to go places he'd never before been.

The West facing wall of his apartment collapsed, exposing the bronze glowing face of the double moon, now covering the entirety of the sky. He stared into the planet, coming in with the burning brightness of a full moon. He no longer needed to imagine anything, he'd reached the point, the grand finale was approaching and could not be stopped.

A crack formed in the ceiling. All across the horizon the city had turned into shaking heaps of rubble and fire. Milt closed his eyes, he pumped and pumped unaware of the cracking and popping, oblivious to the falling ceiling or the shatter and crumbling Earth at large.

The atmosphere sucked away, a concussive wave of forced sped around the world like a shattering stone, turning everything to dust in its wake. He just needed two seconds, one second longer and... he let go. He was filled with blinding light, not from the Double Moon but the pure white light from the other place where he felt everything and he was everything and now he never had to go back.

Ryan Priest is a black American who now lives in the mountains of Colorado after a stretch as a screenwriter in Los Angeles. For a list of his movies and stories please visit www.RyanPriest.net.

SCENTED OILS LAID UPON THE HEAD OF A MORIBUND CHILD, *OR* THE WATCHMAN

NOAH LEMELSON

As the last of his caravan passed under the second arch, the Watchman raised his hand. In sequence his men removed the blinders from their heads, placing them in the jars of diluted rose oil that hung from their horses. The Watchman had not needed to wait so long to give the signal, the caravan had passed the last ruins of the Flaunting Times several miles back, but caution must be set by example. It was a lesson he had taught me well.

The band descended the limestone-marred hillside. There were eight in total, myself included, with the Watchman leading the line. The two closest behind him wore long crimson coats, and—at the back—two more lifted unmarked banners of gray, wearing similarly unadorned masks. The dress of those in-between bore no effect on Congruency and, as such, were a mix. I wore cowhide and a heavy winter cloak of wool to protect against the wind.

The town below had been assigned no name, so far out title was deemed a risk of Dispropriety. It was a moderate-sized confluence of hovels, arranged in an elongated circle, streets shooting out the center like spokes on a buried wheel. Each structure was colored by the dust of Congruently barren fields, no doubt a source of discontentment and a possible cause of Dispropitious behavior, the Watchman most assuredly surmised. For I concluded as much; and I am not yet as keen as he.

The Watchman halted his caravan at the edge of the town, where a bridge overcrossed a dead river. He took his timepiece from his coat pocket and studied its ticking hands as a crowd both curious and anxious formed on the other side. The Manual of Congruence expounds upon the importance of an entrance. If, in entering the town, the Watchman invited Dispropriety then his purpose was made null... or worse. So, the caravan waited.

With an idle finger, the Watchman led my eyes to the bridge itself: a rare act of pedagogy. Old and rust-bitten it was, untouched by paint. On its truss hung fourteen ornaments, three of dog bone, three of wood carefully marked by Congruent icons, five of metal, and the last three irrelevant as long as they were not constructed from material collected from the ruins which hide beyond the hill rims.

The bridge itself was a relic of the Flaunting Times; but one that, by glint of fore-wisdom or mere chance, had not produced Dispropriety. As such, it was allowed to remain standing; though no doubt many villagers feared the Watchman had come to take even this away.

A click of his timepiece and the Watchman waved his hand. The crowd split a path and the caravan marched into the town.

"The mistakes of the Flaunting Times are three-fold," I had whispered once to the Woman Who Had Shared My Bed.

"*Individuality*. No machine can function without the precise compliance of each of its parts. The individual must be disciplined, instructed, made subservient to Congruence."

She had given me a smile. Then a touch on the elbow, careful, like one inspecting a glass statuette.

I continued: "*Growth*. Growth pushes beyond boundaries well kept. Growth leads to knowledge of Dispropriety. It is in our hidebound ways that humanity had lived through centuries, it is through enclosure that we shall still survive."

To my lessons, long memorized, she made a tilt of her head. Her hair hung loose with beads of carved willow woven in. She leaned back on her straw-stuffed pillow, less awed than bemused.

"*Ignorance*. Like a child beyond their parents' eyes who reaches into the flames, humanity must be burnt to understand the danger. That any survived the Flaunting Times was mere Congruency by accident. For those left who catalogue and categorize, Dispropriety may be found and banished just far enough."

I finished, unsure of whether to continue. It was neither Congruent nor Dispropitious to do so, so I merely stared.

The Woman Who Had Shared My Bed stared back, and then opened her bent mouth, as if to whisper soft, but instead chuckled. "And do you think me ignorant?"

The Watchman wore a sharp-topped hat of felt with short rims and coin tied around its base. His face was shaven, his glasses uncracked. His coat was lined with mink fur, but looked an undecorated brown, its buttons flat and unmarked. His boots, too, were simple, and by his belt lay the holster to a small handgun, which he touched softly with gloved hands.

The forewoman stole nervous glances at him as she led the band around her town. Most under the Watchman's orders were not directly assigned to his work, but instead bore rifles, mere muscle brought to maintain order. Congruence could be painful, and though the wise might understand that Dispropriety would be worse, the pain inflicted today might seem unpreferable to the crowd than the unknown terrors tomorrow.

"We have the windcatchers set in a grid," the gray-haired forewoman said, gesturing to the thin metal flags of mesh. "The streets in our square are kept clear after sundown, the candles lit on aromatic nights. The well is drained during winter, and our children never wander beyond the edge of the hills' ridges." The forewoman pointed up to the tip of the valley with the edge of her cane. There stood giant canvas sheets, blocking off from view any peak of the old ruins.

The Watchman's lips bent up in the shape of a smile. The crowd around whispered and murmured, the Watchman's guards held their rifles close.

"Water that is gray in color is buried," the forewoman continued. "We burn all cracked pottery. Our garments are woven with three strands of goat hair or, if for birthing women, four strands."

The Watchman maintained his smile and again took out his timepiece. He ignored the prying eyes of the forewoman and instead counted silently to himself. She, for her part, kept quiet for a time. Then, when the murmurs of the crowd rose too great and the sweat over her brow sat too heavy, she asked: "What are you here for?"

It was Congruent that she ask first. With a click, the Watchman put away his timepiece and gestured. I alighted my horse and removed from its back a carved oak box. With a key from my pocket I unlocked it, and the Watchman pulled from it a bag, woven in the same canvas that marked the edge of the town. He reached in with gloved hand and pulled out a tomato.

"This was traded at a market twelve miles west of here," the Watchman said.

The forewoman stared down at the dirt. "Many towns grow tomatoes."

"The trader was quite clear about the source. Look. Look!" He spoke with such force that he did not need to grab the woman's chin. She inspected the fruit at a cautious distance. From three angles it was normal, from the fourth a yellowish mass of veins could be made out, pulsating every few seconds. From Dispropitious marks oozed a clear liquid that dripped onto the dirt, where it sizzled and smoked.

The Watchman placed the tomato back into the bag. I placed it carefully back into the box. The forewoman said nothing but led silently to the farm.

To be a Watchman, one must assist a Watchman with his work. One must follow and observe his actions, must read the Manual of Congruency, must keep notes on any possible sources of Dispropriety.

I had spoken about this with the Woman Who Had Shared My Bed. This was not in itself Dispropitious but I should have known better.

Her hair was a hazel brown, her eyes a light green. She worked as a carpenter's assistant, like me was still in training. She chuckled more than laughed, and her chipped tooth gave her smile a friendly imperfection.

"It doesn't sound so tiresome," the Woman Who Had Shared My Bed had said.

I did not respond. Not out of anger, but in truth I had not compared my work to others. Such did not fit Congruency. She took my silence as a source for mirthful mockery.

I had met the Woman Who Would Share My Bed when we first passed through her village. The village had had a name. The woman had had a name. They do not anymore.

The tomato farm was between two likewise structured farms of wheat and barley. The plots sat in neat rows, with exception in the middle, where a series of Congruent icons dangled from a five-armed pole. Great canvas sheets hung strung up at the farm's edges, and mirrors sat placed among the crops at regular intervals.

The Watchman inspected the mirrors in turn, as the farmers lined up. Each of the sun-cracked men wore wide brimmed hats, and each carried with them a cut bough wrapped in marked pigskin, all following Congruency. Their gazes were sodden with fear as the Watchman measured the mirrors by string and protractor, wiping the surfaces clean and studying the glass for cracks.

As the Watchman worked, several of the guards lounged and spoke. Their words were quick and light and so I did not join them. Though I was nothing yet, when I would approach they would quiet, fear in their eyes of this small man, this man who might dissect their words, might study their dress, might find hidden Disproprieties that needed resolution.

Instead I practiced the craft, leaving the Watchman to the most important work and instead studying each red bulb and wide leaf. Healthy and plump—by most measurements; a few bug-eaten but nothing worrying.

How naïve they looked, how harmless. Yet there was not a single object in the world, no stem, no stone, no seed that was not at risk of breaking the barriers of Congruency.

The Watchman sucked in his breath and all eyes were upon him. He moved quickly, following the sightline of one of the mirrors, and stopped before a small plant. A gesture of his hand, and I ran over.

There stood the offending sprout, normal from three angles, wrong from the fourth. The Watchman took his pouch a canister and poured from it a mix of two parts salt, one part sand. As he did, I took a match from my pocket. He pulled out his timepiece. After three seconds, I lit the plant.

It burned quick, fire spreading to the edge of the salt. I watched as the flames burned high, a pillar of spinning orange. The smoke floated aimlessly, up above the canvas barriers into that ever-brown sky.

None spoke. None dare open their mouth. The farmers shook, the gunmen stood with gazes glazed.

The Watchman turned and pointed to the mirror. "Whose duty is this?"

"Why did you choose to be a Watchman?"

It was a terrible question for the Woman Who Had Shared My Bed to ask. I should not have answered it. I should not have allowed her to ask it. If I had the foresight, I would not have asked how she had become a carpenter. But I never asked her "why" and I never used the word "choose."

"I did not choose," I said finally, legs wrapped in sheep wool sheets, chest bare.

She climbed over me, eyes staring down towards mine, inquisitive. My answer was not enough.

"I was skilled," I said. "I was right for it. Or so was thought, I am not one yet, I am still a nobody."

She laughed. "My nobody."

I pulled myself up some and shook my head. Outside crickets creaked, and the smell of burning tallow wafted in from the cracked window.

"If I fit, I fit, otherwise it is against Congruency," I explained. "I cannot choose whether to breathe, I cannot choose whether to eat. We must do as we must do, or else perish."

She leaned on me and closed her moss-colored eyes.

"We can always choose."

I should have corrected her.

The Watchman inspected several rooms before he picked out the most Congruent one. I took notes, studying the unadorned wall of the storeroom, counting the stones of the floor, noting their makeup. I used an old machine to measure the moisture in the air, and came to the same conclusion the Watchman had made with a few glances.

I set up a table and placed three candles as the forewoman's men brought in the offending farmer. He was a thin man, with a mottled face and eyes that darted without rest. Not unusual for the town, or any town, nothing in his manners or his clothes suggested Dispropriety. They tied the man with a single rope round his chest and through the back of the chair, which was weighed down by several bricks. This was irrelevant to either Congruency or Dispropriety but would keep him seated. He stared at me, and my gaze gave him nothing back.

The Watchman sat on the other side of the table. He took out his handgun, loaded it, and placed it on the table close by. The farmer glanced at the weapon that sat just beyond his arm's length. The Watchman took out his timepiece and, eyes on the farmer, turned its dial—*clickclickclickclick*—before placing it in the middle of the table.

"Why did you move the mirror," the Watchman said, his voice dull but flung with force.

"I didn't," the farmer replied.

"Why did you move the mirror," the Watchman repeated with the same tone.

"I didn't," the farmed protested.

"Why did you move the mirror."

"I... I don't know who moved the mirror," the farmer said. "I did not see. Did not notice."

"Why did you move the mirror."

"We all adjust them, as the season passes, as Congruency demands," the farmer said. "Maybe someone made a mistake." He had not realized that his answer did not matter.

"Why did you move the mirror," the Watchman said.

"I didn't!" the farmer shouted.

"Why did you move the mirror."

The farmer glanced back and forth. He had not realized that the Watchman had never asked but merely made his statements as Congruency demanded.

"I... didn't."

The timepiece clicked. I lit the first candle.

The Watchman made no sound, but stared—unblinking—at the farmer. He did this for a few seconds, then near a minute, before the farmer muttered.

"I didn't do it."

I struggled to hold still my expression as the farmer turned to me, then again to the Watchman.

"I've done as the Manual said. I've worked hard. I maintain Congruency. I'm a good man."

Silence.

"Do you hear me? I'm a good man!"

The timepiece clicked. I lit the second candle.

"Your father was a trader," the Watchman said suddenly. "Your mother worked fermenting cabbage."

"Why are you—?"

"You assisted your mother, as a proper son. One day your father returned, upset, something in the quiver of his mouth. It was that, as he had traveled through the ruins, his blinders had slipped off. He saw something he did not mean to. He should have closed his eyes, had his companions retrieve his blinders, but instead he stared. He stared a long while, and when he returned home there was something in the quiver of his mouth."

"How do you know this?"

"You asked him, as a proper son, what was the matter. Your father, who had always been gentle, took his fist to you. He hit you, then hit you again."

"We were content..."

"You mother came to grab him and he turned to her. Your mother was a strong one; 'arms of an ox' your father used to joke. If it came to that, she could overpower the man. And yet she did not. For she saw something in his gaze, something that did not induce anger. Nor fear, not in the traditional sense, not fear for her life. There was something about your father that was not him, that could never be him, never have been him, and yet, and the same time, was so clearly him, woven so deep as to be inseparable from the man she had known."

"It was one time. They burned him for it," the farmer said, his eyes to the floor.

"Yet the image came back to you. Year after year, not the fear of your father, not the pain of his fist, but the sight of your mother, the look of her gaze. This you thought on, dwelt on, so deep in your mind that you did not think it strange. It was this, on some sun-soaked afternoon as you adjusted the mirror, which your mind gave focus. What had she seen in her husband's eyes? What had slumbered behind that sightless gaze? And so, you did not check your work. And so, Congruency was lost. And so, Dispropriety found its way in the form of a tomato."

The farmer moved his mouth, but no words came out. He started to quiver, first at his extremities, then the whole of his form.

"Who told you this?" he asked.

The timepiece clicked. I lit the third candle.

The farmer started now to moan and shake. The Watchman stood.

"They were the Times of Flaunting," he preached. "And in those days men knew nothing, desired everything, and wandered unmoored as shattered slivers of glass on a lake's surface."

The farmer tried to ask what was happening; instead, he groaned and rattled against the chair.

"Dispropriety found its way in through a million windows," the Watchman continued. "It found its way into every word, every flip of the wrist, into every idle gaze, and with it, They came."

The chair creaked from the motion; the form of the farmer writhed and stretched, turning bone pale. He looked at me for a moment, and I knew not how to read his warped expression.

"The world was Theirs, for we had abandoned it, and forests turned to deserts, farms to dust, cities to ruin."

The man, if he still was one, opened his mouth, to beg or to curse, shaking all the more.

"And we must Watch then, to see that what remained remains, that which survived, survives."

The thing that was the farmer shook back and forth, screaming sounds that did not fit its mouth. The binding started to fray, the chair started to crack.

"So says the Manual."

The farmer leapt forward. The timepiece clicked. The Watchman picked up his handgun and fired.

I never told the Watchman about the Woman Who Had Shared My Bed. I never told anyone about her question. Or the other questions, the musings, the theories, the ideas. How strange they were, how intoxicating.

I said nothing that first trip. Nor the second. Nor the third when the air was wrong, where the whispers were many in the alleyways, when the Watchman told me that we may soon again have to return. It was selfishness that kept my tongue silent, it was fear, fear that I would have her no more.

Yet he must have known all the same.

The townsfolk burned the farmer with proper Congruency. The body was wrapped in dried reeds, adorned with the proper markings. The remains of his head were covered in a tar, which took quick to flames and smoke.

There was relief in face of the forewoman as she watched her people bury the char and bones. They had only lost one this time.

The Watchman did not stay the night, there was no need, and there were still more towns left to visit. As his band mounted their horses, the wind began to pick up. Waves of dust blew down from the hillside, borne in some distant ruins, mixing with the ashes of the farmer, as the canvas sheets flapped and fluttered on the bluffs. The caravan rode slow up the hill, and as it reached the second arch and I begun to unscrew the lid to retrieve my blinders, the Watchman turned to me.

He had a look on him, one he had given me before. On the fourth trip to the village where the Woman Who Had Shared My Bed had resided. On the trip that had come too late.

Congruency had been long lost by the time we had arrived, Dispropriety oozed from every mouth. The huts lay twisted in odd shapes, the people writhed more than walked, the crops were rheumy and swollen.

It had not been enough for one matchstick, for one corpse to be burned. The Watchman and I took flame to the village, to every hovel, wall, and farm. The guards raised their rifles and let fire upon any that tried to flee.

Among the biting flames, I saw running forms inhuman; unleashing screams that were so very human. I had not stopped to wonder which form had been the Woman Who Had Shared My Bed.

It was not Congruent to wonder.

The Watchman had given me a look, then, as the flames grew high, as the shrieks peaked. It was the same look that he gave now as we crossed into the ruins, leaving behind another body. It was a knowing look he shared, but one without judgment, without condemnation, without even the expected sternness of a preceptor. He bore no anger in his face, nor was his expression one of concern, or even fear. If he bore any emotion in that flat look, it was pity.

For he had not chosen this either.

Noah Lemelson is a young speculative fiction writer working out of Los Angeles. Noah received his MFA in Creative Writing from the California

Institute of the Arts in 2019. He is currently in the editing process for his first published book. You can find updates and more of his published stories at Noahlemelson.com.

DARK WATER

LILLIAN CSERNICA

I'd been working in the parking kiosk by the beach for about a month when I started to notice little things. Clumps of seaweed spaced like footprints leading up to the edge of the sand in front of the kiosk. Seashells piled by the bench where I ate a sandwich before my shift. If I walked all the way down to the breakers, I'd find something washed up there, a diver's watch or a sports bottle or some other useful item.

At first I figured I was just lucky. It kept on happening, and only to me. When I asked the guys on the day shift if they'd noticed anything weird, Chuck and Dave gave me funny looks and laughed, telling me I was crazy. Maybe they were right.

The kiosk sat at one end of the lot, next to the exit lane. Tuesday night I chained my bike to the rack behind the kiosk then stepped inside and set my book bag on the shelf under the counter. On the back of the door was the bulletin board. A memo from my supervisor Roy was thumbtacked to it, reminding all of us to check the far corners of the lot. We'd had trouble in the past with homeless people sleeping over, kids necking, people doing drug deals. Lately I'd been avoiding those corners. They were closest to the beach, right where I'd find the seaweed tracks. Now I'd have to go all the way out there.

I turned my chair sideways and faced the cars. The radio and my textbooks would keep my imagination busy. Only a few people came in and out of the lot. Roy had warned me how slow it would be Monday through Thursday nights. That was all right with me. The shorter junior college summer schedule meant tests were already coming up.

When the fog rolled in it blurred the parking lines just enough to make the kiosk feel like an island about to be swallowed by the sea. At closing time I had to check the lot for any last cars and hang the chain across the entrance. That meant walking all the way out to those corners. I felt a queasy flutter in my stomach as I stuffed the kiosk's flashlight in my jacket pocket and stepped outside.

The waves crashed against the beach. They sounded louder, closer. All that stood between them and me were a lot of empty parking spaces. The fog was so thick it stuck to my face like spiderwebs. The salt taste made my stomach churn. I settled for shining the flashlight's beam into the far corners, looking for the red gleam of tail lights. I didn't see any, so I circled back around the kiosk to the entrance. I fastened the clasp at the end of the chain to the pole on the other side of the entrance, then started walking back toward the kiosk.

The chain rattled. I spun around. Through the misty columns of light thrown by the streetlights, a thin shadow floated toward me. A hand, long-fingered and bony, reached for me. I jumped back.

"Have I startled you? Forgive me." The hand was attached to an older man wearing a blue blazer over a gray sweater and slacks. His smile was friendly, but the angle of the streetlight hid his eyes. "I'm William Corbett. My friends call me Bill." He sounded like one of my professors. "I take it you're the new night man?"

"That's right." His hand was still out. I shook it. "Jim Thompson."

"A lonely task this is, but fine if you like the sea."

"I don't."

"No? What a pity. May I ask why?"

I shrugged. If Chuck and Dave thought I was nuts, I'd better not tell anyone else. "I just— I feel like it's coming to get me. That's all."

"How sad. The sea is your friend. Your brain swims in it with every pulse of your blood."

That thought was so repulsive I clenched my eyes shut against it. Bill chuckled.

"I suspect you have a touch of thalassaphobia. That's the morbid fear of the sea."

"What do you know about it?"

"Quite a lot. You see, my wife was just the opposite. She loved the sea, and it loved her." His voice hardened. "It loved her to death."

"Oh. Well. I have to go now." I backed toward the kiosk.

"Are you tired of being a slave to your fear? I can cure it."

That stopped me. "Are you serious?"

He pulled a gold card case out of his breast pocket, opened it and held out a business card. I took it. He had a string of letters after his name, the address of an office in the expensive part of town, and three phone numbers. I recognized one.

"You work at North Valley?"

"On a consulting basis. Students are referred to me when their difficulties fall under my specialty."

"What's that?"

"Anxieties and phobias. Rather a lucky coincidence that we met, yes?"

"I don't know. I mean, I can't really afford—"

"Please." He held up one hand. "Thalassaphobia is relatively rare. I'd welcome the opportunity to learn more about it."

"You really know something that will work?"

"We can certainly give it a try. Say tomorrow night, after your shift?"

"Okay."

"Until tomorrow, then." He walked off across the parking lot.

I stared after him. The clothes, the fancy card, all those degrees.... He had to be for real. Maybe I did have this phobia thing, but at least I wasn't crazy.

My Wednesday shift crawled by. The stink of the sea reminded me of my old Biology text, making me think of the nasty little monsters that live in coral reefs. In the back of my mind I'd always thought something evil lurked down in the dark water, waiting for a chance to grab my ankles and drag me under. Its fishy lidless eyes watched me. Now I knew there was no monster. It was just this phobia thing.

By ten-thirty the lot was empty. I fastened the chain across the entrance and hurried back to the kiosk, keeping an eye on the blurry shadows. Bill was waiting by the door. He pulled a flask out of his jacket pocket and handed it to me.

"Take a good dose of that."

I took a sip. The Scotch burned a trail down my throat and warmed my stomach.

"Now," Bill said. "Let's get you out where we can do you some good."

He led me along the empty boardwalk and up the pier to the railing. Bill stared down at the water, then up at the stars.

"It's a marvelous world we live in, Jim. The more we make friends with it, the more it reveals its marvels to us."

"Some marvels I'd rather not see."

"You have to confront the fear before you can conquer it." He stared out at the water. "The sea waits to conquer you. Any slip, any carelessness, and it will strike."

"You mean... your wife?"

"We were out in the Caribbean, on a friend's yacht. Rosalind insisted on going for a swim." His breath hissed out between his teeth. "The seaweed trapped her. Before I could dive in and cut her free, it was too late."

"How awful." The weird look on his face made me nervous.

"The sea embraced her like a lover." He glared down at the waves. "A cold, merciless, demanding lover."

I backed off a step. That snapped him out of it.

"Let's get started. Close your eyes and listen to the water. Can you hear the breakers?"

I nodded.

"They crest, and break." His voice eased down to a deep whisper. "Crest, and break. Just like your breath. Feel the rhythm of your breath, Jim. Sink into it."

I listened. My breath slowed until it matched the sound of the waves. I still felt edgy, but more about Bill than the water.

"Listen to the tide, Jim. Listen to your heartbeat, pumping all that salt water through your veins." His voice rolled over me, heavy and soft. "Hear the gentle tide inside your body, and the gentle tide outside it too. All the same, Jim. All the same. Your heart and the sea's, beating together."

I listened, feeling calmer.

"The sea is your friend, Jim. You do want to be friends with the sea, don't you? You want to be happy and calm, like you are right now."

"Yes..."

"Reach out to the sea, Jim. Show it you want to be friends."

My right hand moved a little. I thought of Bill's wife trapped in the seaweed, and those seaweed tracks outside the kiosk. I tensed up again.

"I can't."

"Tell me why, Jim. Why does the sea frighten you?"

The answer came out before I could stop it. "I keep finding things. Little stuff, just shells and tracks in the sand and little presents. I thought maybe they were for somebody else, but it just keeps happening. I mean, am I paranoid or what?"

"Not at all." He didn't say anything for a minute. "That's how it always starts. The sea gives, but it always wants to be paid back."

Before I could ask him what he meant, he pushed me closer to the rail.

"I suspect your fear of the sea might be just a symptom of something deeper. Think, now. Think back to when you were a little boy."

His voice weighed me down again, sending me back through memories. I remembered salt stinging my eyes and a bad taste in my mouth as I threw up. Then it all came back. I was six, at the beach. My father hoisted me up over his head and carried me way out into the waves. We were both laughing. Then he threw me in. I kept fighting my way to the surface, screaming for help. Dad just stood there and yelled at me to swim. Finally my sister swam out and carried me back to shore. Old shame and anger flooded me, hot and ugly. I shoved away from the rail. Bill's hands on my shoulders kept me there.

"I'm right here, Jim. Everything is fine. Tell me what you're thinking."

"My father— he thought it was so funny. He threw me in and left me there." Tears welled up, choking off my voice. "I was screaming, thrashing around. He just stood there laughing."

"I see. Could it be, Jim, that your real problem is your rage at your father? You're really afraid of what might happen if you turned that rage loose."

I stopped straining backward. That made sense. My sister and I weren't allowed to get angry at Dad, could never show any sign of it. I started to cry harder, feeling stupid and awful and better all at once. Bill patted me on the back.

"You've achieved quite a breakthrough. All that's left now is to replace your old fear of the sea with good associations. When I tell you it's all right now, you'll have no fear of the sea at all. Understand?" I nodded. "Wake up now."

Bill snapped his fingers right in front of my face. I jerked back. My eyes opened.

"There now," he said. "Have a look at the water and tell me how you feel."

I glanced at the water, shrugged. "No problem."

"Excellent. Shall we try again tomorrow night? We'll have an opportunity we must not miss."

"An opportunity for what?" There was something about his smile, a manic eagerness, I didn't like.

"The moon will be full. The power of its light will chase the darkness out of the water and cure your fear."

That didn't sound like anything I'd read in my Psych texts. "Sounds more like magic than psychology."

He gave me an odd look, then laughed. "There's a little of both in each."

Something still bothered me. "I can see how Dad being a jerk started all this, but what about the stuff I keep finding?"

Bill waved that away. "It's probably nothing more than a mild delusion. You wish your father would apologize, perhaps by giving you toys. Since you can't confront him directly, you've transferred that wish to the sea itself."

That made a strange kind of sense. "Look, I'd really like to thank you for your help. Can I buy you dinner or something?"

He shook his head, smiling that same disturbing smile. "Tomorrow night will settle a number of debts."

The next night after closing I met Bill at the end of the pier. Over his sweater and slacks he wore a poncho of black silk. Seagull feathers, fish bones, chipped seashells and bits of colored glass decorated it. As I got closer I could see silvery symbols embroidered onto the cloth. He had on a necklace of cowrie shells. A flat circle of mother-of-pearl hung off it. More symbols were scratched onto that.

"Hey, Bill," I said. "What's all that for?"

"The Orb of Dreams and the Sphere of Conquest stand side by side in the heavens, with Venus suspended between them. On such a night can miracles occur."

"What are you talking about?"

He blinked at me, then chuckled. "Psychodrama. Shamans have been curing people with it for thousands of years."

He made it sound perfectly natural, but something about that get-up bothered me. He'd put a lot of time into it, so he couldn't have made it just for me.

"First, a toast for luck." He handed me his flask. I took a swig. The Scotch had a peculiar gritty edge to it. He probably got sand in the cap. I handed it back.

"Now watch the water," he said. "See how it swirls. Follow it, around and around. Sink into the rhythm of the water. Feel it in your breath, in your blood."

The Scotch filled me with its bracing fire. The heat moved out of my stomach and along my arms and legs, up into my head. My tongue felt thick. My eyes swung back and forth with the current. The swirl of the water wobbled and blurred.

He pulled me away from the rail and made me sit on the bench near the stairway that led down to the fishing platforms below the pier.

"Stay right here." He hurried down the stairs.

Something was very wrong. I tried to stand up. None of my muscles even twitched. Hypnotism was supposed to make you suggestible, but not turn you into a robot. What had the old man done to me? The scotch. It had to be whatever made the Scotch taste funny.

"Please." Bill's voice came from right below me. "I've waited so long. The stars, the tide, everything is in place."

The waves hit the pilings. I heard a hiss like steam shooting out of a bad radiator.

"Haven't I served you? You've taken everything, my youth, my love, my life itself!"

A slow hiss answered him.

"You thought you'd trap him with your petty trinkets, didn't you? You'll have him, all right, but only if you give me what you promised!" Bill hurried up the stairs and put a hand on my shoulder. "Come along, Jim. It's all right now."

I felt no fear of the water, but I was terrified of him. Even so, my body stood up and followed him. I felt like an engineer trapped inside a runaway train. I took one step after another down to the slimy, barnacle-crusted platform. It rocked a little with the strength of the rising tide. Bill grabbed a fistful of my jacket and jerked me right up to the platform's edge.

"Come here, Jim. Look at the water. Let it see you."

The water down here was dark, dark enough to smother the moonlight, dark enough to make every one of my coral reef nightmares come alive. My heart nearly pounded a hole right through my ribs. I begged my frozen muscles to run.

"Luna and Venus link arms in the heavens," Bill chanted. "Lovers return from graves long filled. The gates of death swing wide on hinges oiled by blood your priests have spilled!"

A larger wave sloshed onto the platform. Little wavelets ran toward my shoes. Nodding, Bill cackled. He made a paler shadow against the dark water. The bits of glass on his poncho glittered at me like lidless eyes. Those fishy lidless eyes. . . . Raw panic exploded inside me. Straining as hard as I could, I dragged one foot back from the edge.

Bill stared at the water, looking confused, then furious. "Here he is, just as I promised. Now give me Rosalind!"

The water did nothing but stroke the toes of my sneakers. Bill growled and thrust a hand under his poncho. He pulled out a fishing knife and reached for me. The waves heaved beneath the platform. My one moving foot skidded in the slime and I fell over. Bill staggered backward, teetering on the platform's edge. A wall of dark water rose up behind him. I stared at it, praying it was only the drug in the Scotch making me see things. Anything else meant this was real. The dark water crashed down over Bill. For a second I saw him trapped inside it, slashing at the water with the knife. Then it sank. I dragged myself to the edge of the platform and watched Bill disappear into the gloom. He fought all the way down.

I rolled over and sprawled on my back, still sluggish. The panic screamed at me to get away before the water grabbed me too. I tried to sit up. A stronger wave splashed across the platform. Something rattled. It was Bill's cowrie shell necklace. Another present, from the sea.

The waves lifted the platform again, gentler this time, like they were rocking me. I touched the necklace with a cautious fingertip. The sea had never hurt me. That was just my father being a jerk. The dark water had saved my life. I sat up and dropped the necklace down over my head. The mother-of-pearl circle gleamed. My heartbeat slowed, beating in time with the waves that kissed the pilings and drew back like shy lovers.

The sea was my friend.

At age five, Lillian Csernica discovered the *Little Golden Books* fairy tales. From there she moved on to the works of Ray Bradbury, Harlan Ellison, Tanith Lee, and Terry Pratchett. Her first short story sale, "Fallen Idol," appeared in *After Hours* and was later reprinted in *The Year's Best Horror Stories XXI*. Ms. Csernica has gone on to publish over fifty short stories in such markets as *Citadels of Darkover, Fantastic Stories, Killing It Softly,* and *After the Happily Ever After*. Her Christmas ghost story *The Family Spirit* appeared in *Weird Tales* #322 and *Maeve* appeared in #333.

Historical fiction has become Lillian's favorite genre. Fans of steampunk will enjoy Ms. Csernica's Kyoto Steampunk short stories appearing in *Twelve Hours Later, Thirty Days Later,* and *Some Time Later* available from Thinking Ink Press. Ms. Csernica's two nonfiction ebooks, *The Writer's Spellbook: Creating Magic Systems for Fantasy* and *The Fright Factory: Building Better Horror,* provide nuts and bolts instruction in the techniques of writing those genres.

Born in San Diego, Ms. Csernica is a genuine California native. She currently resides in the Santa Cruz mountains with her her husband, two sons, and three cats. Visit her at lillian888.wordpress.com.

Margaret Lets Her Self Go

Samantha Bryant

"She's really let herself go." Margaret heard the whispers of the two women as she passed them in the grocery store. She wasn't sure who they were, though she had this vague idea that she'd known them once, before she'd found the orb. She wondered if she had liked them, if that comment would have stung her then. She couldn't remember. It certainly didn't matter now.

Let herself go. That was one way to look at it, she supposed. She knew they meant that she looked sloppy or unkempt. People spent a lot of time worrying about surface details like that. It was true that she wasn't spending time on external things here lately. It was hard to give up precious minutes for things like teeth, hair, and clothes; things that would be gone in a scant eighty or so years, just like the rest of her body. Sooner, if things went as she had planned. Maybe much, much sooner.

Let her self go? Would that she could! In fact, she resented the minutes this trip to the grocery store was costing her. What discoveries were going unmade so that she could keep this unwieldy machine functioning a few more days, feeding it protein and caffeine just so it would keep moving. What a delight it would be to let this paltry self go.

In a few more days, she wouldn't need it anymore. Her work would be complete and she could leave the awkward sack of flesh behind and live amongst the stars with the other practitioners of the art. Soon she really would let her self go. There would be no need to be an individual. There would be no self, only the collective. She would never be alone again.

For now, though, she would have to keep her body going and that meant finding something to give it energy. Not wishing to seem like she was lost, she moved quickly through the store, trying to look like she was looking for some particular item. Really, she was just looking for an empty aisle, so she could give herself time to think without calling attention to herself. At last, she found one.

Stopping in the center of the aisle, Margaret stared at the rows of colorful cans on the shelves before her. She realized she couldn't parse the labels. It was as if they were written in a language she didn't understand. Or like they had a spell on them that kept her from being able to focus on the text. She pursed her lips and considered. She used to know how to read this language, she was sure, but now she couldn't remember what sounds the symbols were meant to represent. Her mind was given over to the language of the people of the orb, who spoke only in resonances and frequencies, without the interference of written symbols. If only the cans could sing their contents to her heart like the orb did.

She decided to choose one at random. She liked the colors on the tall, cylindrical containers. She picked one up. She felt nothing. No vibration in her palm. She studied the container again. There was a picture of a dog on it. That didn't seem right. She also didn't see how it opened. Maybe she'd better choose another one.

The short, flatter containers had a ring on the top. She was reasonably sure that a person was intended to pull on the ring to get to the contents. She liked the beautiful curls in the text, too. She put a few of those cans into the shopping cart. Moving quickly again, she grabbed a bag from another shelf. It didn't matter to her what flavor these various foodstuffs were. She would only need this body a few more days. Surely anything would work to keep it functioning that long.

She pushed the cart up to the cash register, remembering to wait for the man in front of her to put down the plastic bar before she started stacking her cans on the moving belt. She was nervous. Harold had done the grocery shopping ever since her breakdown. It had been years since she'd been in a grocery store.

But she had thought her way through it step by step. She knew what to do. Standing in the line, she patted the small bag that hung from her arm, reassuring herself that she had brought the right things. She had brought some of the green paper so valued on this plane. Silly really. The whole idea of exchanging labor for paper and paper for goods just struck her as ridiculous. It would be a relief to be past such petty negotiations.

Margaret bounced on her feet, fighting her growing impatience and practicing her lines. It was important to respond appropriately to what the girl said. She hoped she could recall how to form the words. It had been several days since she had spoken aloud. There had been no need, when she could just commune with the people of the orb, mind to mind, soul to soul. Without Harold, there was no reason to use her voice at all. The inside of her mouth felt dry and rusty.

"Hello, Mrs. Stevens. Did you find everything you need?" the girl asked.

Margaret forced her head up and down and smiled. "Yes?" she said, hoping that was the correct response. It must have been, because the girl started moving the cans across the light, making them beep. The beep startled Margaret. It sounded like the danger warning from the orb. But surely there could be no danger from the Others here. She gripped the dagger in her pocket just in case.

"I didn't know you had a cat," the girl said.

"A cat?" Margaret had no idea what the girl meant. But she had observed that you could just repeat what you heard and people would move on. It had worked at the bank when she went to take out the money. She didn't want to get trapped here, talking to the girl. It wasn't important to recall the details of language when she was so near ceasing its use altogether. She just wanted to get back home and finish her preparations.

The girl was looking at her strangely. Something was wrong. What had she missed? She smiled again, forcing the corners of her mouth up and trying to hide the panic that was rising in her like bubbles from the lungs of a drowning man.

It worked. The girl smiled back and laughed. Margaret echoed the sound, though she had no idea what might be funny. Humor had never been easy for her, even before the orb. Now, it eluded her completely.

"You always were a trip, Mrs. Stevens," the girl said, shaking her head.

"A trip?" Margaret repeated. Was the girl asking about her journey? No one was to know that she was leaving. Secrecy was paramount. If they knew, the Others would try to stop her, keep her from getting to the seventh plane. The orb had sung her the warning song, and she understood that the Others wanted lower beings kept low. The people of the orb were heretics in the eyes of the Others because they valued the lower beings, choosing to raise beings from all the worlds in all the planes.

Reaching into the deep pocket of her loose pants, she gripped the small dagger again, the handle sliding into her palm with an easy familiarity. She bit the inside of her cheek hard enough that she drew blood. It tasted strong in her mouth, strong and right.

Then the girl announced the amount of green paper that she wanted. Margaret relaxed her grip and let the dagger slide back into the pocket, unused. She had stared at the papers for an hour before coming to the store. She was sure she knew which symbols went with the words. She passed two pieces of paper to the girl and waited. The girl fed the papers to the machine in front of her, then took out other papers and some small round pieces of metal Margaret recognized as coins of this land. She held these out to Margaret, who took them cautiously, and slid them into her bag.

Margaret shuffled forward to the end of the table where the girl was holding out the bags and when Margaret took the bags, the girl touched her arm. Margaret nearly pulled the dagger then, but something held her back. The girl leaned in and said, "It's good to see you getting out, Mrs. Stevens. Give my best to Mr. Stevens."

Margaret blinked, a big smear of wetness sliding down her cheek. She wiped at it with the back of her hand, trying to understand what it was. Were the girl's words a sort of spell that could pull the liquid from her body like this? She backed away a step. She couldn't afford the influence of any dark magic. She was nearly finished with the purification rituals. They wouldn't take her if she were contaminated. She grabbed the bags and nearly ran from the store.

"Poor woman!" she heard the girl say to someone as she moved towards the doors. "She's never been the same since their daughter died. She'd be lost without Harold Stevens. That man is a saint."

Lost? She wasn't the one who was lost. It was Harold who'd come untethered from this plane. But she had not lost him. She was sure that was where he had gone. She would cross over to the seventh plane and he would be there, waiting. Why else would the orb have begun to glow and sing right as Harold's shell had folded in on itself and crumpled to the kitchen floor? If it wasn't a signal, then what was it?

Glowing with the success of her mission, Margaret walked the few blocks to her house. The sun seemed to kiss her skin and she could hear music in the breeze. It echoed the humming of the orb. She increased her pace. She needed to get back to the circle before the alignment was past.

As she approached the house, the music grew louder. It was like the bones and tissues of her face had picked up the signal and were rebroadcasting the notes in her flesh. She felt her body lift, almost as if it actually grew lighter. She paused at the edge of the fence to calm the giddiness. She noticed again the dusty blue car parked in front and she knew that it was hers to use, but she hadn't felt sure of how to operate it. It seemed safer to walk. She couldn't risk injury or death when she was so close to opening the pathway. If she didn't make it across, Harold would be lost to her indeed.

Right after he crossed, she had thought she might be able to pull him back, but he had loosened his hold on his body too completely. The invisible ties that would have guided him back to that particular house of flesh had snapped. She had been wholly unprepared for the suddenness of it. She didn't even have the right herbs on hand, had not studied the rituals or purified the Circle. She had thought they would have years yet.

Stepping up to the door, Margaret muttered the words that would disable the protection spells she had put in place to ensure that the Others did not interfere with her work while she was out. As she stepped across the threshold, she felt the pressure bubble release then fill back in behind her.

Moving quickly, she set the bags on the table with the other items that had accumulated since Harold's crossing. She had to push over stacks of paper, but she found space for the new purchases. Free from her burdens, she turned and hurried to the central room.

Grateful to have found the Circle intact, Margaret closed her eyes and sent thanks to the people for protecting her work from interference in her absence. She knelt on the golden cushions and ran her hands over the sacred objects, letting them sing their harmonies into her hands. It had taken a while to collect them all. The herbs were laid out on the silver platter, the candles waiting in the glass bowl. The coins of many lands were organized in the proper pattern around the center ring. All was just as it should be.

Finally, she rested her hand on the small white orb. It hummed against the palm of her hand, reminding her of a small animal. Was this what the girl had meant when she asked about a cat? She thought she recalled a similar thrumming coming from a creature with oddly shaped green eyes, some time in the Before. She warmed to the vibration now, feeling reassured that all was still well.

Returning to the bags on the table, she pulled out one of the cans and popped the tab on top. The contents did not please her nose, but she ignored that. The physical senses were not important. The information they conveyed was often false and unreliable. Even while her nose objected to the strange lumpy looking contents of the can, her stomach rumbled, demanding to receive it. Conflicting signals like this were part of what made her want to escape the trappings of the flesh and move to a higher plane. Food, bathroom, sleep. Mundane concerns, of no interest. Not when there was the possibility of transcendence.

She stuck her fingers into the soft, mushy meat and sucked it into her mouth. She nearly gagged, but she forced herself to move the nutrients around in her mouth then swallow them down. She would definitely not miss having to do this when she was free of this corporal plane. A few more swipes and the can was empty. She quickly consumed two more cans, wanting to ensure that her work would go uninterrupted until she could finish the rituals. The rumbling in her stomach ceased, though it was replaced by an unpleasant roiling sensation that made Margaret worry she would lose yet more time to dealing with the needs of this awkward machine. For now, she would ignore it and return to her work.

She stood studying the dining room wall where she had hung her charts and tables. All signs pointed to a window in the next few days, but she still felt uncertain. Harold had been so good at interpreting the more ambiguous cross references. She wished she could consult him. Then it struck her. If Harold was in the seventh plane with the people of the orb, she could contact him, just as she had contacted the people.

Returning to the Circle of High Resonance she had constructed, she lowered herself to the floor. She wrapped the golden ribbon symbolizing her tether to his plane around one wrist. The other end was affixed to the floor itself. Taking a few deep breaths, Margaret focused. She concentrated on shutting down her senses.

Vision was both the easiest and the hardest. Simply closing her eyes would stop her from seeing anything, but the mind would insist on creating its own images: the reddened, panicked face of Harold as he realized he would not be able to come back; the cold, stiff, painted one they had made for Angie. Wrestling the images down was hard work, but she was determined. Finally, she achieved a visual blankness, a perfect blackness against which she would paint her pathway to the Seventh Plane.

After her vision was under control, she worked on hearing. Even alone in this small shelter, Margaret was accosted by sound. Clicking and ticking sounds abounded, despite the removal of all the time devices she could find.

There was kind of skittering in the walls that she worried might be the Others, having discovered her work and trying to break through the protective spells. Even her own body made sounds she could hear in the darkness: a wheezing from the nose, a buzzing in the ears, the pulsing of blood moving through her limbs. She concentrated on the low hum of the orb until it was all she could hear.

In the silent darkness, Margaret strove to release scent and taste, the twin senses that tethered a person in the lower planes. The food so recently in her mouth made this difficult. Perhaps she should have rinsed her mouth. But if she got up now, she would have to start again. So she persevered, concentrating hard enough that she began to sweat.

Finally, it was only the sense of touch holding her bound. This was the hardest to let go. The other senses shut down, she was painfully aware of the sensations of the flesh. The hips complained about the position she maintained. The skin seemed to crawl, whether from warmth or some other cause, she didn't know. She focused intently on the black empty space she had created in her mind, trying to let go all awareness of the physical.

She reached out with her mind to the People of the Orb, calling gently with her heart's song—Ha-rold? Ha-rold? She persevered, even when she met with no response. She called his name until the words became a chant without meaning, a string of nonsense syllables —haroldharoldharoldharoldharold.

Finally, she felt it, an answering vibration. She didn't open her eyes to look, afraid to break the spell, but she knew that, if she had, the orb would now be glowing and floating, its soft light filling the shelter with purity and life. Her mind was awash in a green glow, and through it she could see Harold smiling at her. He was holding hands with Angie. Angie, all smooth and bright again, not mangled and broken. Neither of them spoke, but seeing her, they turned and held out their arms to her. She could almost feel the warmth of their embrace.

"How?" She begged instruction. A vision appeared. The kitchen calendar. She saw the red markings on the calendar. Three days hence, on the confluence of threes. The anniversary. Margaret nodded. It had a nice sort of synchronicity. It made sense.

She concentrated, asking directions. Harold's crossing had been unexpected. She had been making preparations for them both, but then Harold's essence was absorbed so suddenly. How would she follow? The directions came in flashes of images. Then she could see Harold and Angie again, their smiles glowing white as they faded into the starlight.

Wilting, Margaret dropped her head to her chest, the connection fading. She wiped her wet face on the sleeves of her shirt. Angie had been so beautiful, perfect as she had been before the car had crumpled around her, and Harold looked so happy. His face was open in a way she hadn't seen in years. No worry clouding the corners of his eyes. No sadness pulling his shoulders down.

Three days. Only three days! She was so excited and, at the same time, so scared. Now that the day was named, she should feel relief, but she found the relief was intermixed with other, complicated emotions. Margaret took a deep breath. There was no time for doubt now. If she didn't cross over soon, Harold would have moved on without her. He could only stay in the interstitial plane a short while.

Margaret stood, wobbling unsteadily on her feet. She had hated this body for so long. The way it ached when the weather was cold. The heaviness of it. It had felt like a prison her lighter soul was unaccountably bound to. Yet now, thinking of truly letting it go, she found she had some affection for the old thing after all. She would miss the feeling of her hair wound through her fingers, the texture of a soft blanket against her skin. It had served her well, this fleshy holding cell.

Looking down, Margaret noticed the odd stain in the center of her shirt. That would have really upset her once. She remembered that she had a fondness for this particular garment. Harold had told her that she looked beautiful in it, that the blue jewel-tone complimented her eyes. She also noticed that she did not smell pleasant. Her body's scent was almost offensive.

Absently, she turned and entered the bathroom. She reached in and turned on the hot water in the shower, waiting until it filled the room with steam, then turning the temperature down to a level her skin could withstand. She pulled the stained shirt over her head and dropped it into the overflowing hamper, grimacing at the feel of her matted, greasy hair against her fingers.

Stepping into the warm stream of water, Margaret was overwhelmed by the sensation of the drops bouncing against her flesh. How long had it been since she washed this body? Too long. Once, she had enjoyed long showers. Harold would come knocking after half an hour and ask if she was ever coming out. She'd say she couldn't, there was still hot water left. Raising her face into the stream now, Margaret wished Harold would come and scrub her back. That was another reason to miss the body: touch.

Stepping out, she pulled a towel from the shelf and wrapped herself in it. She felt wonderful. She pulled down a little tub of something pink and smoothed it over her skin, releasing a scent of flowers and fruit into the air. It was a good first step, a purification for the ritual. She ran over the details of the vision Harold had sent her, making a list of items she would need. She was pleased to realize that she should be able to find everything in the garage or the house. No more trips to the outer world would be necessary.

But first, she wanted to check on Harold. It wasn't Harold anymore. She knew that. But it still brought her comfort to be near the shell that had once held him. Still wrapped in her towel, she went to the room that had been Angie's. It didn't look like Angie's room anymore, but, in her heart, Margaret could still see the pale green curtains that matched the and garden mural she and Angie had chosen when she was thirteen. Harold had painted over it, trying to make it look like not-Angie's room, but it hadn't helped.

As Margaret entered the room, pain gripped her mind and blinded her for a moment. She leaned against the doorframe waiting for her vision to clear, pushing down the dark images that threatened her focus. The Others were always trying to bind her to this plane with pain and loss, but she would not give in to them. Harold and Angie would be there waiting. They would all be one with the stars.

Harold's shell was laying on its back. It had been difficult but she had dragged it there from the kitchen and pulled it onto the bed. Now, she sat on the edge of the bed and rested a hand on one of his hands. A liquid feeling rushed up her arm, washing over her like a wave in a sun-warmed lagoon. "I wish we could have crossed together, Harold. I'm so scared, going alone." She let her gaze travel up the body to the face. It was still frozen in an expression of surprise and joy, mouth agape and eyes wide. She smiled down at him, and stroked his face, smoothing down his hair. Soon she would see for herself what had surprised him so.

Returning to their bedroom, she opened the closet and looked for something to put on. Clothes seemed a silly thing to be concerned about in the face of eternity, but her flesh was growing cold in the towel. She wouldn't be able to concentrate if she were shivering. Maybe the body knew its time was short and wanted its comforts for the end. Searching through the clothing that crowded the enclosure, Margaret felt worry rising in her again like an ill wind. It was no simple matter, getting to the seventh plane. There were so many planes, and if she miscalculated, or missed any aspect, she could end up in a different plane than Harold had.

Pulling a soft purple sweater over her head, she was attacked by a sharp and sudden doubt. How was it that Angie had been there, too? Angie had made no preparations to choose a plane. She had simply died when the truck had destroyed her car. She shouldn't still be in the seventh plane, the Waiting Lands. She should have moved on by now. Had Harold somehow called her back from the Upper Spheres so she could serve as an additional beacon to guide Margaret's way? Or could it mean that the Others were manipulating her vision for their own ends, trying to keep her from making it?

She sank to the floor, her body shaking. There had to be a way to be sure. She saw the sun's rays coming through the high window that illuminated the closet space. Morning already. One day gone. But there were still two days. She had to be sure. She ran to the living room and dropped to the floor in front of the small pedestal the orb sat on. She forced herself to calm down before she let herself reach for the orb. Any other element could be replaced, but the orb was unique. Without it, all hope was lost.

After wiping her hands on her pants to ensure they were not sweaty or slick, Margaret reached out with two hands, forming a cup with her palms. With her fingertips, she coaxed the orb until it rolled into the hollow of her cradling hands. Instantly, it began to glow, the bright whiteness casting colorful shadows on the walls through the cracks in her cupped hands. Margaret let her head fall back, and pulled the orb to her heart. She felt her rapid pulse slow and come into sync with the pulsing of the orb, just as it had the first time the people had reached out to her.

When she opened her eyes again, she could no longer see the room she knew her body still rested in. Instead she was in an eddy at the center of a sea of colorful light. She recognized the colorful swirls of light as the people. She wanted to look down at herself, but "down" was not really a concept that made sense in this space, just as "self" did not make sense. A light blue swirl of color spun into a corkscrew shape, which Margaret understood as a greeting. She wondered how she was seen by the people. Did she also look like a swirl of color or was "look like" another construct that didn't apply? Maybe the swirls of color were only there to accommodate her, in her limited perceptions.

The time for idle curiosity and exploration was long past. Though the concept of time was meaningless for the people, they seemed to understand her urgency. Trying to push past words to pure thought, Margaret struggled to open her mind to the probes of the people. There was pain deep in her head, seated in the brain. Despite her wish to cooperate, something in her physiology resisted the invasion. She'd always heard that the brain didn't have nerve endings. Maybe that meant the pain was psychological, but it didn't make it less real. Margaret gritted her teeth and endured. She had to know the truth of the situation and wasn't going to let pain stop her.

When the probing ceased, Margaret almost collapsed with relief. But she knew there was more to come. She braced herself for the flurry of images. All communication from the people of the orb had been like this: fast, direct, and incomprehensible at first. This time was no different. In quick succession she saw images of Harold and of Angie, from life and their deaths, and where they were now. The image of Angie kept blurring into redness.

Some hours later, Margaret returned to consciousness. She was lying on the floor, the orb a few inches from the fingers of her outstretched right hand. She immediately sat up and replaced the orb on its protective pedestal. She was fortunate that it had not broken. A pounding sound startled her, but she did not drop the orb. The sound came again, and Margaret gradually came to realize that it was someone knocking on the door.

She moved to the window and peeked out the corner of the curtain at the porch. She didn't know the woman on the porch. At least she didn't think so. Seeing that she was raising her hand to knock again, Margaret went to the door and opened it on the chain, peering out. "Margaret?" the woman said. Maybe Margaret did know her, or was supposed to.

"Yes?" she responded cautiously. If she kept her phrases short, the holes in her memory of the language were less obvious.

"I just wanted to make sure you're all right. There were strange lights coming through your windows."

"I'm fine," she said. The woman peered into the opening, trying to see around Margaret. Margaret stood so that she blocked the view of the house.

"Is everything really okay? I haven't seen Harold in a day or two. Is he sick?"

"On a trip," she said. She quickly closed the door and hurried back to the Circle. The orb was still and silent now, but the message had been clear. That wasn't Angie she had seen with Harold.

It was as she had feared. That had been one of the Others wearing Angie's face. Angie wasn't in the Waiting Lands with Harold. It was going to be important not to let her attention become divided when the moment came.

The moment? Margaret suddenly realized that she wasn't sure how much time had passed. While communing with the people of the orb had felt brief, she knew that this was not necessarily so. Time flowed differently in other planes. Rushing to the television, she turned it on. A small box in the corner showed the date and time. Parsing the numbers took some effort, but when she realized what they said, her panic was immediate. It was a matter of hours until the window closed.

Flinging the plastic remote, she hurried to grab the remaining elements to complete the ritual and moved back to the Circle of High Resonance.

Moving quickly, but with a sureness she seldom felt anymore, Margaret removed her clothing and made the ritual cuts in the flesh of her wrists. She lay down, resting the orb on her abdomen, and let herself go blank.

There was a blue flashing light that seemed to reflect in the glass of the windows and bounce around the room. The door burst open and a large shape in a coat filled the doorway. It was one of the Others, Margaret felt sure. Closing her eyes, she lifted the orb in her cupped hands toward the sky. The ceiling seemed to slide away until she could see the whirling cosmos above. She felt the orb begin to spin in her hands, then lift away, filling the room with its pure, white glow. Her body lifted into the air and took on the same bright glow. She felt her atoms spread out into the darkness, streaking upward and upward, until they intermingled with the people. All feeling of Margaret dissipated like so much smoke. She was one with the people. The Others couldn't reach her now. She had let her self go.

Samantha Bryant writes the *Menopausal Superhero* series and other women-centered speculative fiction. You can follow her @samanthabwriter on Instagram and Twitter or check out her website samanthabryant.com.

THE MAN WITH NO EYES

CHRISTOPHER MALENEY

The first time we went to Holy Trinity, I thought I was going to die. Looking back at it, I almost wish I had.

A year ago, I guess. Maybe more. Time passes strangely now. We went to Holy Trinity because Mom insisted. She went twice a week, before she got sick, and, "If you're going to live with me, you're going to have to be a Christian."

If I'd had a choice we wouldn't have gone, but Morgan liked the idea, and Morgan usually got her way.

The two of us shuffled into the pew. A bunch of people came over, hugging Mom, shaking her hand. Saying all kinds of stuff, "Oh, so this is your daughter." I wonder what they thought. I wonder what they'd heard. A fuckup. A prodigal child. Maybe, a vet. Hell, why not all three, the way they looked. One half with delight, one half with disgust, but they all looked shocked, no matter how well they hid it.

Mom had insisted on the dress, even if it did show the tattoos. I hate wearing a dress. Morgan, however, ruled the day and the dress was worn. At least it was black, even if it did have strawberries on it.

It was high summer. The AC was on, but it wasn't doing much. The church was hot, and close and uncomfortable. I didn't like any of these people. They were old, mostly. Old and ugly. Or the real plastic types who go their whole life looking middle aged.

After, I don't know, ten minutes or an eternity of people socializing, they started playing music and everyone quieted down. The choir started singing about God, and about how good God was. How the Holy Spirit was going to come down from God and fill us all. How we would go out into the world and spread the Spirit to all the people, and lift them all up to heaven. It didn't do much for me, but people seemed to enjoy it. They were tapping their toes and clapping their hands, looking around in expectation.

As the music crescendoed, the doors at the back opened and everyone burst into cheers and stamping, hollering approval. He was dressed in an immaculate suit with a plain, white tie down his front. He was short and, from where we were standing, I couldn't see much of him or what he was doing, but the people kept clapping and the music kept playing.

People were getting up and moving to the front, coming back full of shaking excitement. I thought at first they were kissing his ring maybe, but then I saw the dollar bills they tossed into the basket at the pastor's feet. With every new donation, spasms of worship roiled the crowd, shaking them. Voices shouted, "Testify," or "Praise God."

Morgan seemed to be drinking it in. She smiled, watching them go. With each new height of ecstasy, she seemed to relax a little more, sink into her role. Smile. Then Mom leaned over and whispered, "Here, go give him this."

It was a crisp, hundred dollar bill, neatly folded. She never gave us money, and now here she was throwing a hundred dollars away on some faker. But Morgan smiled and said, "Of course."

I wonder a lot about Morgan. Does she not mind people staring at her? As we walked up the aisle, with all those people clapping, staring, I wanted to shrink down into nothing, but Morgan just smiled back, hands clasped in front.

Up close, I got a look at him. Reverend White was a small goblin of a man. His smile stretched from ear to ear, exposing perfect white teeth and pulling the creases on his wrinkled face into a contorted caricature of human emotion, but his eyes didn't smile. Deep-set and blue as ice, they scrutinized. They watched, observed, and calculated with all the warmth of a distant winter star.

Morgan dropped the money in the basket and scurried back up the rows to Mom. Behind us, the music crescendoed again, with pianos and drums all smashing together, the chorus leader warbling, and the crowd all cheering and shaking. Then, Reverend White said into the microphone, "God is good, my children. God is good."

The whole audience erupted into cheers, crying, laughter, and, "Amen, amen."

"Oh my holy children," he cried again. "Here we see the goodness of the flock. Here we see the fruits of God's charity. Are there any here tonight who have not felt the measure of God's love?"

Everyone swore they had felt the measure of God's love.

"We are all God's children. And, as a loving parent, God sends his love to all of us. His love makes miracles. His word makes us free. Did He not send His Son to us?"

"Yes, yes He did," the audience shouted.

"Is His Son not Jesus, the Redeemer? The one who makes the blind to see, and the lame to walk, and the dead to rise again? Does He not move through us, and with us, and in us?"

At each question, the audience screamed and hollered. They raised their hands and shook them. The hot, still air was humid with perfume and sweat. Morgan looked around, trying to decide how and if to join in. Mom was going at it with the rest of them, testifying with all her might.

"We are here today in the presence of the Lord. We are here today with the Holy Spirit. We are here today as a community of God's love and God's love is in us all. Can you feel it, children?"

The choir was doing its best impression of the angels. Couldn't tell if they were just intoning syllables or if they were saying real words, but their voices echoed from the speakers strategically placed around the church, concealed in the huge potted plants. Their drone threatened to overwhelm; and Reverend White's voice booming over the music only added to the effect.

"Who is willing to receive the Spirit? Who is willing to receive God? I can sense you out there. Come and be healed, my children. Let us all be healed."

A man in the first row stood up and shouted something. Reverend White turned to him and stretched out his hand. The man fell back into the arms of those next to him. "Be healed," Reverend White commanded.

From the other side of the church, an old woman, supported by a walker and the arms of her grandchildren, approached Reverend White. He turned very suddenly to her and waved his hands. The old woman stiffened, then started to jerk and kick. Reverend White did a kind of pulling motion and the woman began to jump and dance, laughing as she did it. Her grandchildren laughed with her, all dancing together.

"Hallelujah," Mom shouted in chorus with the others around us. "Testify."

"And are there some here," Reverend White spun to face the main body of the audience. "Are there some here who are new to our congregation? Bring to me the neophytes. Bring to me the errant sheep, recently returned to the flock. Bring me the nonbelievers, that they might witness the power of the Lord."

"Well," Mom turned to me. "Go on then."

I wanted to shout, "Me? You dragged me here you old witch," but Morgan just nodded.

"Anything you say, mother."

I don't know how long I have to write this. I only have little moments of control. I think the rest of them are sleeping, but can't be sure. Maybe worse than that.

Don't know where we are. Motel. Somewhere south, maybe west. It's hot and the sun warms the asphalt outside to near boiling.

I grabbed some pens and paper from the clerk and I'm writing this in the bathroom. Feels safer here. Small room, but solid.

How long have we been here? Days maybe. The man with no eyes has some business in town but the other two won't let me know what it is.

Have to start at the beginning. Where is that? Or when? These threads spinning off into has been, will be, will have been. Keep losing my way.

Where did I leave off?

At least I wasn't the only one up front. One was a tall man, balding, with pink skin, who smiled disarmingly from behind bifocals. The other was an old woman who was gazing at Reverend White rapturously.

He approached the old woman first. "Good morning, mother. What is your name?"

She whispered shyly into the microphone held by one of the ushers, "Theresa Vincetti."

"Theresa, a lovely name. A holy name. You have come for your grandchildren, isn't that right, Theresa?"

"Yes, Reverend," her face lit up. "How could you—?"

"Prophecy is a gift of the spirit, Theresa. To those who believe, all things are possible. They have fallen into wickedness, isn't that right? Is it drugs?"

She nodded, and whispered something, but the microphone didn't pick it up.

"What was that? Ah, yes. The curse of our sinful age. Never fear, Theresa, here you will find refuge. Already the hand of God is moving towards them. They shall pay for their sins. In time, they will come to you and beg for forgiveness."

"Oh, thank you, Reverend. Thank you."

"Bless you, my child." He then turned to the man and asked him, "How are you today, Peter?"

"I'm fine," he started, but then stopped. "How could you—?"

The crowd laughed and whooped. An old party trick, I supposed.

"You're here with your wife, aren't you Peter? She has told me of your troubles."

"Forgive me, Reverend. I was weak. But now we can't pay."

I wondered what it was. Embezzlement? Infidelity? It seemed strange to have confession so out in public, but maybe it was all part of the grift. Shame and forgiveness are a heady combination.

"It is good you came to us while still you could. For your wickedness, you have been punished. But never fear, Peter. God is merciful, and he is just. By the end of the month, your fortunes will be restored. I have seen it."

The crowd gasped. Voices shouted, "Testify," from the back. "Amen."

"We have all seen the goodness of the Lord," he addressed the crowd. "We know His love. Wealth and security are nothing for His believers. Only believe, and the Spirit shall move through you, and God will reward you for your belief. And what's your story?" He turned so rapidly I could've jumped. But Morgan was ready.

"Casey O'Connor, Reverend. I'm here with my mother."

"That's right," he nodded. His face was a mask of sympathy, but I could see his eyes. They were the same as mine. Bright blue and utterly empty. "You've caused her a lot of grief, haven't you? But you're going to be better now. Now you'll be a blessing to her. You'll be baptized anew in the Holy Spirit." And he stretched out his hand.

I've always wondered, how do people do it? Are they faking it, or is it psychosomatic? Do they actually believe that some magic force moves through these charlatans? Not until that moment had I ever considered that it might be real.

Maybe Morgan faked it, but I could swear I felt something shove us. We were launched backwards, landing on the carpet. And long streams of laughter emerged, erupting helpless to mingle with the chanting, wailing cries of the congregation and the choir, ascending to heaven.

I don't know how much the others know, or even if they're still there. They won't talk to me. Operating behind enemy lines in my own head. Moscow Rules.

Awoke in a different city. Different motel. Heading somewhere, just can't tell where.

After that first session, we went every week. A whole long summer of Jesus on the weekends and at home. Days I got to spend at the mall, selling T-shirts to the kids with money to buy them. Then home to soaps and the evening news.

I wasn't even suicidal anymore. It all felt close enough. The soul was being chipped away and I knew it would be only a matter of time. But then...

The sequence of life's events is a strange, impossible thing. Decisions lead to situations. At the church, they'd call it God's Plan. I hope it's not.

If part of God's plan involves bulldozing forests to make room for shopping malls then I say God's an asshole. And if God's plan involves keeping Mom sick so that Reverend White would give me a job so that...

If this is God's Plan then I hope it fails. And if God controls all our lives then I hope I end up in Hell. I've seen God's agents and I'll take my chances with the devil, thanks.

"My children, like it or not, we are in the middle of a war." It is Sunday. Reverend White is speaking; we are in the fifth row. Mom is breathing heavily. Morgan is into it, hands gripping the hymnal we have just finished singing from.

"This war is invisible but it is constant. We are surrounded by the enemy. From time immemorial, Satan has walked among us here on earth. He is a wicked tempter and an unfair fighter. His weapon is the sly whisper in the unguarded ear. His knife drips with foul poison and his tongue is forked.

"Everywhere in the world we are beset by the weapons of the Enemy. His words croon from the radio. Our children wear his slogans on T-shirts. And the television is his greatest invention yet, allowing him to preach every hour of every day in any language we can understand.

"But simply avoiding the word of Satan is not enough, my children. By affirming our faith as Christians, we are marked out. We are watched for any opening. And even in the strongest heart there will be cracks; in the most faithful soul there will be doubts. We must be strong and ready our bodies and our souls to do battle with the Enemy. But who is our Enemy?

"The book of Ephesians tells us, 'we do not wrestle against flesh and blood, but against principalities, against powers, against the rulers of the darkness of this age, against spiritual hosts of wickedness in the heavenly places.'

"Our enemies can take on many shapes. In their true forms, they are almost invisible to the eye. They are beings of shadow, and darkness. But we can see the forms they create for themselves. And we can see what they make of their hosts. They are the parasites of the world, and their life cycle is predictable, once it is understood.

"First, children, their words infect the mind. In this stage, they are laying the groundworks for their invasion. The host begins to question the Word of God. They may be conned by magicians, or by sceptics. They may be tempted by vices, their guilt assuaged by secular humanists who say, 'everything is permitted, for there is no God.' But we know these are lies.

"In the second stage, the host is demonized. They hear voices. They may hallucinate. Their dreams are filled with depravity and their daydreams take on the fantasy of sin. The demon has invaded the subconscious mind and is taking over the immune system.

"In the third stage, the battle is won or lost. The demon possesses the host entirely, making their will subordinate to that of the demon. From now on, they will spread the word of Satan and attempt to woo all around them to the same level of corruption."

97

Morgan gave a small snort; but managed to turn into a suitable gasp by the time Mom looked over. She flashed a look of warning before turning back to Reverend White.

"Though the demons are strong, my children, the power of God is stronger; and through Him we may overpower and dispel these demons once they are discovered. It is our job to remain vigilant. Be wary of any corruption in your hearts, or in your communities. We must put on the armor of the Lord. Pray for those who cannot, or will not, see. And remember to donate to the cause."

He paused to gaze over the crowd with his gleaming smile. They burst into a thunder of applause that Reverend White grabbed, summoning them up from their seats. "Now, children, let us turn to page sixty-five in the hymnal and raise our voices in praise to God, the Most High."

Casey was a good kid. She liked dinosaurs and Egyptian mythology. She wanted to draw comic books when she got older. But things have a funny way of turning out.

I never met Casey. All I have of her are the scraps of her life pieced together. There are drawings, and journals, and books with stamps in them. Then, when she was eight, it all stopped. The others don't talk about it much. Did Casey vanish then... or later? I don't know. Introspection is searching for whispers in a haunted house.

I awoke on a hammock on a forty-eight hour R&R in Honolulu with some girl. I don't remember her name but I remember her deep brown eyes and the brush of her lips on mine. She asked my name and I told her it was Noelle; and ever since then, there I was. Self-actualized on a one-night stand.

And so, I'm left with a suitcase full of questions. Why join the army? When did Casey leave? My skin, interwoven network of scars and tattoos, tell a few stories; but they aren't mine. I've heard some from Elliott when he's drunk. I think Morgan knows more than she lets on.

I wonder if it's too late now to find out.

But Mom was getting worse. She was tired all the time, coughing up thick wads of dark phlegm she tried to hide. Couldn't.

I told her to go to the doctor, but she was stubborn. Reverend White must have healed her half a dozen times but he said all he could do was keep it at bay.

Morgan said it was fine. I tried to reason with her. Mom might listen to Morgan. She'd never listen to me. I knew better than to try Elliott. So, I watched and waited and then it happened.

She was out in the garden. It was July. We were picking the tomatoes and, in the heat, she struggled. Grasped for breath and missed. Fell down in the dirt. Before I knew what was happening, we were running for the phone.

"Ms. O'Connor, your mother is very sick. She's going to need a lot of help before we can release her. Is there anyone else who we can call to help you with her?"

"No, no," I wanted to say. "It's fine." But I wasn't speaking.

Memories fractured after that. I went to sleep for a while. I'd awaken shaking in the blue night, heat sticking sheets to skin. Walk to the window.

Nightmares followed me then. There was someone else in my house. I had the impression that a hand had been rattling at the door, feet creaking the stairs. Double-checked the chain. I could smell him still.

It had been so long since I'd seen Elliott but I knew his hallmarks. I woke one night to find another tattoo fresh under plastic on the right forearm. A single rose. White flesh tone petals with black outline. Another night, woke to find it colored in.

After church one day, walking with Mrs. Winchester—whose perfume reminded me of Mom's—she was telling me all about her own run-ins with mortality while we counted the magpies on the fresh cut lawn. I don't remember how many. She had a different version of the rhyme from me.

"Seven for the devil, his own self."

We met Reverend White coming the opposite way. It was late summer. The day was unbelievably hot and still. He asked Mrs. Winchester to let us alone for a little while. Then he asked me how Mom was. Wasn't it expensive, those hospitals? Yes, it was. A pity, he said, that faith could not do more. "But God always has a plan for us, Casey. Have you felt God's hand moving in you?"

"Well," I started. I really wanted to pass the baton; but the other two were quiet. Sleeping maybe.

It didn't matter, though. Reverend White continued. "I know. It can be hard, when we are tested, to remain steadfast in God. Have you read the book of Job? 'God's voice thunders marvelously; he does great things that we cannot comprehend.' I think you would find many deep meanings in the Bible. It holds secrets to understand all of existence. But that is not why I came to you today.

"I know that your family is not as rich as, well, some of the others who attend. But your mother is devout. A pillar of the community. I think that there is a way for the church to give back."

"Oh, I don't," I started. "I mean, you don't have to—"

"I want you to work for me, Casey. I can see something in you. Something strong and unyielding, and I think you could be a mighty weapon for God. In return, we will contribute to your mother's hospital bills. It's the least we could do."

"I—"

"Don't thank me now. Just come to my office on Tuesday, around ten. Or, what day works for you?"

"Wednesday works better. But..." I didn't know quite what to say. I was stunned.

"Don't worry," he patted me on the arm. "It'll all work out, just fine. But don't believe me. Believe God. See you Wednesday."

Then he walked away, leaving me gasping like a landed fish.

We get home. Car pulls into the driveway. Feet step up the path. Hand on the door that slams shut behind. Keys jingle in the bowl on the table. Can't honestly say who's piloting until Mom shouts down the stairs and I reply, "Hey, Mom. Just me. Need me to bring you anything?"

"Is there still some of that sweet tea in the fridge?" she calls, voice thin and raspy.

"Didn't Dr. Metzger say you shouldn't have much of that stuff?"

"What that old devil don't know won't kill him."

My hands are already opening the fridge. Pulling out the jug and pouring a glass. I carry it upstairs (tread of feet on that carpet always brings up memories like bile to be swallowed) into the room that smells of flowers and death. Place glass carefully in my mother's trembling hands. Soft fingers curl around it slowly.

I do not watch as she lifts it to her mouth. Look at the pictures on the dressing table. Smiling faces safe behind glass. Look at the chest of drawers' familiar scrollwork. The curtains drawn against the hot sun. Do not think about the black mass gathering in the bottom of lungs, creeping tendrils clawing through frail body. Do not look at the face.

"How was church today?"

"Fine. They said prayers for you. Reverend White..."

"Ahh, that's nice. Good people."

The machinery in the room whirring, clicking. Half hospital, half bedroom. They even took out her wedding bed and replaced it with one from the hospital.

"Is Bob here?" I ask.

"Your uncle has gone shopping. He'll be back ... soon."

"Good." No time to waste then. Up to the room. Lock the door. Make no noise until sundown.

"Casey, you have to forgive him. God would want you to forgive. What happened was years ago."

I turn to the door, announce, "Reverend White wants me to work for the church."

"What? Doing what?"

"I don't know. I'll find out Wednesday." Hold out my hand for the glass. She gives it back and I catch a look. Sunken eyes and sallow skin. Tubes under nose and God I could switch right now but I force them down like nausea. "He says they'll pay some of your medical bills. We'll work out the details later."

"Casey," she tries to say. Says nothing.

Wheels crunch in the driveway and my feet are already fleeing up the stairs to my room.

The curtains are drawn tight against the sun. I am not here. I am not now. I am there and then. Sitting in the dark, sweltering office. Shaft of light peeks in, illuminating dust floating in the still air. Silhouette of Reverend White at his desk. Hands clasped before him. Eyes piercing out from shadowy face as if lit by their own internal light.

"Thank you for coming, Casey. How's your mother?"

Present but not in control. Looking out eyes like a Halloween mask. Morgan speaks for us, "She's stable, at the very least. The pain's not too bad. My uncle's looking after her, and a nurse comes every other day."

"Ahh, that's good. You're a good daughter. Now, we had talked about getting you a job. I suppose you're wondering what I need you to do. But, before that, why don't we get to know each other a bit better?"

"I'm sorry?"

"I just want to hear more about you. Your mother told me a few things but I want to hear from you directly. What are you like, Casey? What are you good at?"

How are we supposed to answer that? Casey was a good kid but Casey's not here anymore. Can I take a message?

"Well," Morgan shifted in the chair. "I've done a lot of things. I work at the mall most days and I've done some secretary work. When I was in California I worked as a waitress. And I spent a few years in the army; but I doubt you need me to shoot something for you," she finished with a smile.

He smiled back, white teeth gleaming in the gloom. "Probably not yet. But, my my, that is certainly a varied career. And where do you see this all leading to?"

"I'm sorry, Reverend, but what is it that you need? I don't mean to be disrespectful, I just wonder where this is going."

"Very well put. The human condition, isn't it? Stumbling in the dark. Wondering where we are headed. Searching for the light that will illuminate the path. One final question, then, Casey: what do you know of spiritual warfare?"

"You mean like what you were saying in church a few weeks ago. Prayer to ward off Satanic influence?"

"Exactly. I suppose, to a certain extent, we want our followers to believe that the cultural struggle, and the internal one, is the extent of our activities.

Certainly shunning Satan and his works, as well as prayer, invocation of the Holy Spirit, worship—these are all useful in the ongoing conflict. But they are by no means the end all be all. Simply that so many of the more important activities are best kept from the public. They could not understand. But you and I, Casey, we are more than sheep. I am a shepherd. And you are a sheepdog. A defender of the pack from the rapacious wolf. Will you take up the holy standard?"

"I'm sorry, I don't exactly follow."

"Never mind. That will come. For now, there is a man I'd like you to call. You have a story that you're going to tell him. Are you ready?"

"What?"

And then he said something in a language I could not recognize. I'd heard Tongues spoken many times by then, and it wasn't Tongues. I recognize it now but then it was just part of the mystery.

I felt serenely calm, but I was no longer just Noelle. I was not Morgan, or Elliott, or whoever Casey had been. I was the chimera. The three in one. And we knew what we had seen. We knew what had been done to us. And we knew what we had to do.

Reverend White's eyes shone a radiant, crystal blue as he held out the phone.

"Thank you so much for agreeing to meet on such short notice," Morgan said, shaking hands.

The journalist's name was Ethan Millay. He had a ponytail and round glasses. Pimples mixed with stubble on his chin. We met at the Wendy's in the mall, crowded in the lunchtime rush. All around us, voices rose and fell in the ceaseless hubbub of human language. The journalist had out his notebook and his phone was already recording. "No trouble, Emily.

On the phone you said it was about the Rose Shelter?"

"Yeah, I was there in the spring. I mean, I've been debating so long telling this story. Thank God, I'm in a better place now. I thought my last boyfriend was bad but then I went there and, my God, you don't know how far a person can fall until you really do, you know?"

"Maybe let's back up a bit. You said you were there in the spring?"

"Yeah, in April. I was with this guy... Jack, if you need to know his name. Anyway, he was just awful. I mean at first he was great but then it just got worse, and he'd say he loved me afterwards but he never stopped. My parents live in Ohio so I couldn't go there, even if they wanted me back. I didn't know anyone here. I just had nowhere to go. And I thought it would be a safe place. Ha."

The journalist was writing it all down diligently, like he really believed. I wanted to scream at him. Didn't he hear the hollowness in Morgan's voice? Couldn't he read her sarcastic smile? Evidently not. "So you went to the Rose Shelter?" he prompted her.

"I'd seen the ads in the paper. Is it suspicious to be advertising a shelter? Maybe not. And I'd seen Dajani on the news—"

"Do you mean Councilwoman Nabiha Dajani?"

"I do, yes."

"Okay, just want to make sure," he said with a reassuring smile. "Please, go on."

"I understand. Okay. So, I'd seen Dajani on the news talking about the good work they were doing and I thought it couldn't be worse then where I was. So, one day, my boyfriend was at work and I packed up my stuff and went."

"Can you remember the date?"

"It was early in April. Before Easter, because they let us celebrate it, though they were all Muslim. I can't remember much more, sorry.

"Well, when I got there it seemed fine. They gave me a bed and a room and explained the rundown. We had classes and counselling and group projects. It seemed really great, until I'd been there about two weeks and the men came. I remember freaking out a bit because men aren't supposed to be in there, but Dajani was showing them around and everything. We all stood at attention and they examined us. Looked at our arms and our teeth. It just all felt so... wrong, you know?"

"But nothing happened at the time?"

"Not unless you count being looked at like a side of meat at the market. I knew I should've talked to a woman about this. I'm sorry, maybe I should—?" she picked up the handbag and stood, but Ethan grabbed her hand.

"Wait, no. I'm sorry. I didn't mean to say... I just wanted to check that, look. We've been looking into Councilwoman Dajani for a while. Your story could help a lot of people. We just need to know. Please, just trust me."

Appeased, Morgan sat again. "Alright. Well, they examined us. And afterwards, I asked one of the women who they were. She said she didn't know, but that they came around every month. It seemed when some of the women's time was finished, these guys would come and pick some of them up. Took them off in black SUVs. Nobody knew, or nobody would say, where to."

"Wow. That's awful." Ethan had a hungry look in his eyes as he asked, "Could you describe the men?"

"There were three of them. All tall, muscled. Wearing suits. Dark sunglasses. They had dark skin. They spoke to Dajani in some Persian or something. They all laughed a lot, but it wasn't nice laughter you know?

"I didn't wait around to see what they wanted. I ran away, and stayed for a few weeks with some friends. As soon as I knew they weren't looking for me, I came to you."

He finished scribbling his notes, and then looked up. He either didn't notice or didn't care about any of the inconsistencies in the story. Working for the Daily Star, he'd heard his share of crackpots I'm sure. It didn't matter. The story sold.

The next six months passed quickly. Mom didn't get better, but she didn't get much worse. Having quit the job at the mall, we worked for Reverend White almost full time now.

It started with small things. Following a Rabbi to a motel. Calling the cops on a union leader's house. Planting drugs on a teacher at the community college. Slowly, it escalated.

I think Morgan liked it, was the thing. We were making money and we were helping the church, which she started to view as more than a grift. But I think what Morgan most liked was getting away with it.

My room is a mess: clothes on the floor and cups on the desk. Elliott folds his clothes and he makes his bed every morning. I've never been in Morgan's room, but I imagine it as a series of increasingly complicated traps and puzzles before you reach the final room, only to realize too late that it's only one last trap and the real room is further in.

Six months of it. My memories are untrustworthy at best. We broke into a Catholic church, I know that much; but what was uploaded onto their computer, I don't want to remember. Breaking into a storage unit, but why, and who with, I don't know. I switched in once, on my back in a strange hotel; I don't know the man's name, but I saw his face again when Morgan sent the photos to his wife.

All I could tell myself was that it was for Mom's health. But at a certain point, you can't believe your own bullshit anymore, and all you have left is inertia to keep you going.

"You have proved yourself an invaluable asset. Not only to the Church, but to God as well. In six months, you have done more to aid this sin-ridden community than many have done in their whole lives. As you saw today, our congregation has more than doubled since you began your holy work. Just today we made over twenty-five thousand dollars. Soon, we'll need a bigger church," he giggled.

We were in the green room. He was behind a small screen, taking off his makeup, changing from his preacher's suit and tie to his socializing suit and tie. Two ushers stood in attendance. Morgan waited without fidgeting.

"There is someone I'm going to introduce to you today, Casey. He is, like you, a holy warrior. My most trusted captain in this war against evil. Together, we've been watching your performance. He agrees with me; it's time for you to be promoted. The war is ceaseless, Casey, and you will be a mighty weapon for God."

We walked over together, across the lawn. Springtime and all of life was beginning. The day was warm but not yet hot. The trees had decided it was safe to offer up their buds. The future was at hand.

The crowd parted for us. Men and women, coffee cups in hand, gazed with awe at the Reverend. They murmured greetings and thanks. A few approached with last-minute donations. He returned their favors with blessings and an open palm.

We approached a trio of well-dressed couples. A bald man in a gray suit that shouted ex-military left off his joke and said, "God bless you, Reverend."

"And you too, Tom. Mary. Hello all." They murmured respectful greetings, and Tom fixed his attention on me. "Tom, this is the candidate I was telling you about. Casey O'Connor."

We sized each other up as we shook hands. He was tall and broad-shouldered. Tough hands with thick fingers. Sunburned pale skin was a sunglass tan. He smiled with perfect teeth, saying, "Hi, I've heard a lot about you. Reverend White said you've been doing some work for the church."

Elliott responded for us, fortunately, "That's right. Simple stuff, really. He told me a bit about you, too."

Whatever dumb test the handshake had been, we passed. Tom relaxed his grip. His wife, a plastic blonde in a tight blue dress, took his arm and smiled. Her smile was as fake as it was wide. "Oh, you must tell us all about it. I think it's just so great what you men do. Fighting God's war. There's just so much evil in the world these days."

Reverend White answered quickly, "Casey mostly works as a courier of sorts. He was the one who found the Ninevah shards I mentioned in today's sermon. Records of the actual edicts of Solomon."

The other men of the group took Reverend White up on this. The women were more interested in discussing the evil in today's world.

"It really is an age of sin. You would not believe what I saw this week. Two dykes in the middle of town. Just walking around like it was perfectly acceptable. Well, I tell you what I did—"

I was actually relieved when Tom tapped me on the arm and nudged his head. I followed him outside.

"Tell me about yourself, Casey."

Elliott has a different stance from the rest of us. He spreads his legs a bit more, and his shoulders are taut. I can tell he likes wearing a dress even less than the rest of us, but he passes it off okay. "What's there to tell? Served in the 25th in Afghanistan, then again in Syria. Came back a few years ago, kinda drifted. Then I found Jesus through a buddy at the VA. Now I work for Reverend White and take care of my mom. Just trying to be a part of God's plan." I wonder if Elliott believes that. I know I don't. It doesn't matter, though. What's important is that Tom buys it.

"Did Reverend White tell you what we're gonna be doing?"

"No, he did not."

Tom takes a drag from his vape pen, filling the air with cotton candy clouds. I wished I was smoking a cigarette. "See, Casey, there's three types of people in this world. There's the sheep; that's most of the people inside, good, ordinary people. Then there's the wolves; killers, rapists, Muslims, you name it. People like you and me; we're the sheepdogs. We keep back the wolves. But, here's the thing: not all the wolves are people. Do you read me?"

I must've heard the sheep-sheepdog bullshit a thousand times before. Elliott was nodding along like it was new information, but the last part hit all of us. "What...?" Elliott started. "What, like actual wolves? Or, no..."

"I mean demons, Case. Devils. Malignant spirits bent on destroying us, dragging our souls to Hell. Turning this world to ash. Their agents— some are, I think, unaware of what they're doing. But our job is to stop them. Reverend White thinks you can be an asset. Do you?"

"That's ... Wow." I could feel Elliott stumbling. Tongue-tied.

"It's a lot to take in. There's not always much we can do. Prayer can only go so far. Purify with fire's the best way, usually."

"Surely it takes more than fire to kill a demon," Morgan cuts in with a toss of her hair. Elliott sinks back. I can feel his relief. "Prayer. Excommunication. Intercession—"

"We have a mixed approach," Tom assures her. "When you come to the ranch I can go over it in detail. But, suffice it to say, we know what we're doing."

"The what?"

"The church's compound. Our unit trains there. Didn't he tell you? No worry. We'll run some drills. Introduce you to the team. What day works for you?"

He wants something, I can tell. I don't know what it is, but I am afraid.

I think I might have to go away for a while. I hope I can get through all of this before that. If you've read this far, well... Thanks anyway. I'd like to tell you to say something to Mom or somebody but there isn't anybody.

You never see it coming. No matter what it is. We take turns, imagine them as choices, blindly down paths in the maze of memory. Pray we'll get to the middle of it all, but I don't think there is one.

I don't think there's any lesson in all this. What could translate across the vast gulf between those who've looked across the veil and those who've not. I can give you a glimpse of the impossible truth. I don't expect you to believe me. I don't care. I, we, whatever, have been crazy since I was a child. Crazy's just a word used by those who pray their meaningless actions will never take them beyond the shores of the placid isle of comfortable normality.

We approach the end. Here, let me show you.

I don't know what I'd expected from a compound. In my mind was military bunkers of poured concrete and machine guns out the front. I didn't expect a housing development. McMansion cul-de-sacs with SUVs in the driveway. The checkpoint at the gate was the only thing in line with my expectation. Elliott spotted the handgun under the commanding officer's jacket, and a man with a rifle in the house overlooking. Not that we had any difficulty getting in; one look at Reverend White and they saluted, letting us roll through unimpeded.

"I bought this place twenty years ago," he explained as we drove around. "We decided that it would behoove a community of God to have a domain of our own. A haven for the True Believers from the sinful world.

The militia was a natural offshoot. The police are too tied to the mundane world. While it's true that many are of our fold, the Enemy has long infiltrated their ranks. Catholics, atheists, and worse."

I knew better than to talk. Reverend White would eventually burn himself out ranting about the sinful world. I just had to pretend to nod along. Elliott was busy admiring the compound anyway. Strategic chokepoint, fire lanes, the works. Piles of sandbags concealed in the hydrangeas. An APC in the double-wide garage.

"We designed the place for maximum defensibility. Confuse the enemy, that's step one. Most of these houses are lived in by our flock. The soldiers bring their families. But a few of them are not quite what they seem. I'll show you, don't worry," he chuckled, sensing curiosity. "But first I'll take you to Tom. He'll put you through the paces."

Like some vast labyrinth, we coiled clockwise and counter-clockwise through the neighborhood until we reached at last the very center, where an immense church stood, the focal point of all life and activity.

We didn't go in the front, though. Reverend White led us around to the back and in through a storm cellar. Down the steps into darkness, smell of cold stone and damp earth. We were stopped at a metal door. Reverend White dialed an alphanumeric combination on the pinpad and the door hissed open.

"There you are, Reverend," Tom said. "I was beginning to think you'd been spotted by the Enemy."

"The Lord guides my every step," Reverend White replied, shaking hands.

Tom was dressed in combat fatigues. A pistol was strapped to his waist. He turned to me and we shook hands. "Good to see you, Case. Did Reverend White tell you the plan?"

"He mentioned you had some drills you wanted to run. It's been a minute since I last fired a weapon, though."

"Well, don't you worry none about that. We've got time to get you up to speed."

"But what about—?"

"Now Casey," Reverend White said, a hand on my shoulder. "Our community takes care of its own. We will keep an eye on your mother. What we have planned is of vital importance to the war. Surely you won't back out now?"

What could I say? Surrounded by armed men, in the middle of their compound; we'd passed the point of no return long ago. Elliot laughed, "Hell, I wouldn't miss this for the world." I think he meant it, too.

The next week passed in a blur. I came to only rarely, late at night, considering my own mortality and the voices softly snoring in the bunks around me. My whole body ached. I smelled like gunpowder and sweat. New names all around me at chow time and in the rec room: Dalston, Williams, Foster, and Clark. But it was coming together.

In the day we did shooting and sparring and combat drills. The night was for survival and escape. Old instincts re-surfaced. Elliott loved every second of it.

It was nearly summer again. I awoke one morning to the smell of honeysuckle from the hedge outside the window and I knew it was time to go. We were as ready as we'd ever be.

"Today is a good day to be a soldier of the Lord. Every day is a good day to be a soldier of the Lord, but on this day, brothers, we have found our Enemy.

"God has directed our searches. God has picked the battlefield. God has chosen the very hour that we shall do battle, and with God on our side, how could we fail?"

At this, the twelve of us in the church cried out, filling the hall with ringing shouts. Reverend White raised his hands, and we quieted down. "Must I remind you, brothers, of the Sword of Gideon? 'The Lord said to Gideon, go now, and look, for I have delivered the Enemy into your hands.' Surely, there is nothing God cannot do. Surely, we are God's chosen host. And as the three hundred prevailed against the mighty army of Midian, as the walls of Jericho collapsed, as God—our loving and gracious God—has led us to victory after victory, so shall we prevail again. Let us put on the armor of God and go forth; for, with God on our side, nothing can stand against us."

We all hollered again, doing our best to fill the high, empty house with noise. It echoed back to us from the rafters. Then, Tom got up to speak. He had a Powerpoint demonstration showing the maps and diagrams of the attack.

"Reverend White and his acolytes have outlined this building. It's a small warehouse on the edge of the city. Main entrances are here and here, with secondary exits here and here. We will approach as one unit—we've got a man inside, so getting through the gate should be no trouble—and then split up upon arrival. Our approach will come from the south. First Unit will set up a north and western perimeter, while Second Unit takes the south and the east. Any questions?

"Now, our strike team will consist of Reverend White, his two acolytes, plus Williams, Dalston, O'Connor, and myself. Reverend White will locate the heretical artifact, and we will either destroy it, or neutralize it long enough for transport. Understand?"

"What is the artifact, sir?" asked Dalston.

Reverend White replied without standing, "God will reveal the answers as they are needed."

"That means it's need-to-know," Tom re-stated. "All clear? Okay, now the outside team..."

We were in four SUVs, big black things, but they did allow plenty of space. We had an hour long drive, enough time for the thrill of starting to be replaced by the cold anxiety of going. Elliott was taking a pre-mission nap and it had been a while since I'd seen Morgan. All I could do was sit there, bulky in my body armor and rig, smelling of gun oil and sweat, and stare out the window.

Reverend White was next to me in the back. He was staring out the window too, smiling at the countryside that rolled by. There was a question nagging me like a loose tooth. I don't know how he sensed it but he looked over at me and asked over the roar of the big diesel engine, "What is it, my child?"

"Well," I started, not sure of how to begin. "Maybe it's better not to ask. I mean, it's something I should know, probably, but how do you find them? How does God tell you where to lead us?" It was as polite a way as I could think to rephrase the question I really wanted to ask, *aren't you just bullshitting us?* He didn't seem to notice, though.

He flashed his pearly white fangs at me and laughed, "Why, Casey, of course it's natural to be curious. There are many tools in our arsenal, and the one that you ask of is known as 'spiritual mapping.' In practise, it bears many similarities to heretical practice, but it is a gift of the Spirit. Of course, that doesn't stop our enemies from accusing us of witchcraft."

I tried to laugh with him. I think it came out a little weak.

"It begins of course with prayer," he continued. "It is easier with a small group and my acolytes are experienced with assisting me. We pray to God for understanding, for Him to outline our Enemy, their locations and their intentions. Nothing is ever hidden from God, after all. And then, He shows me. I imagine it is like what the practitioners of witchcraft know as 'astral projection,' or 'dream-walking,' but theirs is a pale shadow of God's true power. What it is, you see, is the soul travelling beyond the limits of the physical... and the temporal. In this state, we may be shown one iota of God's knowledge. We can perceive the past, present, and future. Often the significance is unclear, but God's revelation is continuous and His plan is all-encompassing."

"So that's how you found this place? And do you know, then, what we're going to find?"

His smile faded for a second, before redoubling. His blue eyes hooked me, and his words echoed in my brain. "Wait and see, Casey, and all will be revealed."

Dissociation is a strange thing. I stare out my own eyes like a diver from a mask. I watch myself act, but none of it comes from my will. It's then that I feel myself living in some huge and empty mansion, wandering from room to room, hoping to find some trace of familiar resonance. Finding nothing.

Standing on the precipice, awaiting disaster. Crouched in a gas station bathroom scribbling what would assuredly be seen as ravings if only they weren't true. I have seen with my own two eyes. My own two. Is that what he wants? Eyes to see and flesh to dance. What is this place to them but some plaything to be twisted, to be torn apart, and all the juice sucked.

Worms. We are not even worms. We are— no, I don't want to know. Too much already I have seen into that thing's view. I've felt its grip inside my skull and I will fragment like the others. Splinter away into nothing. Who would have thought that I would be the strongest, or, at least, the last. I can only hope it kills me soon. The vessel is nothing. Let it have the flesh.

We walk unwitting on a surface tension. Above, the uncaring void. Below, the gaping maw. Stare at the lie too long and you'll break the skin. And who knows what Hell will then be released?

We approached the warehouse. Easy. Too easy. Nobody seemed to notice or to care. Was he controlling all of them? Why not?

The SUVs screech to halt. We all spring out with guns in hand. Elliott jumped out. Gunsight sweeps over the silent parking lot. The wind whistles in the broken-glass windows, like vacant, staring eyes.

"Come on people," Tom shouts. "Step two, let's move."

Elliot takes the six as planned. Rifle watches the doorway, the catwalks, the rows of silent stacks of crates. It's afternoon. Golden sun glows through the western windows and the shadows are long. Twilight world sunk in gloom.

"Can you feel it, Reverend?" Tom asks.

"It's getting closer. We should be seeing it. Can you feel anything?"

"Yes, yes, but where?" one acolyte responds. The other whimpers.

"Is there another level? Somewhere below?" Reverend White asks.

"I don't fucking—" Tom starts, interrupted.

"There," Dalston insists. He's right. A trapdoor. Williams pulls it open, revealing steps rickety with age. They creak as first Tom descends, then one by one the whole team. We're last. The light is a square frame in the darkness.

Flashlights play on walls. Earth smell. Boxes, barrels. Who keeps things down here, and what?

"That's it, that's it," an acolyte whispers. Tall wooden crate towers over all of us.

"Get that fucking thing open."

Knives out, pop open the sides that fall away with ease. Staring up at it.

"Holy fuck," someone whispers.

White marble glows in the flashlight. It's a man, probably. I know, I remember, it was handsome once. You could see how lovingly the sculptor had carved each muscle, each fold of his robes. For centuries, the people stared at it. Marveled at it. Loved it.

As if I remembered generations of students who sketched it, hoping to discover the secrets of a masterwork. The students who then, in their rapture, withered. The students who wept blood at the unattainable and found release in knives. And with their worship, with their blood, it changed.

But they never stopped coming. Even when the slender fingers seemed to grasp. Even when the upright posture bent, beckoned. Even when the smile widened, and the eyes sunk and vanished. Still, the faithful came. The pure white marble never changed.

AND SO AT LAST YOU HAVE RETURNED, WORM

"Dread Lord," Reverend White gasped. "I have brought you sacrifices."

SCRAPS AND CRUMBS. YOU KNOW WHAT I NEED

"But—?"

DO YOU QUESTION ME?

The noises started then. Guns and flashlights clatter to the ground. Gasping, choking. Elliott's hand at our throat, clawing at the tightening. Throttled voices screaming. One by one, the noises were stopped by a thump on the ground. Then it came to me.

The prison had taken on an aspect of the prisoner but the reality was unspeakably worse.

First, the death-stench. He emerges from the rotten ground, clad in robes of damask and skin, oozing pus from gangrenous wounds. Long claws reach out, wrap around your face, bringing it closer to his own corpse-visage.

His teeth are broken obsidian, his mouth rippling with a maggoty tongue. The nose has been chewed off. But worse is the place where his eyes are not.

Those empty twins. Dark stars paternal to all our unforgiven sins. They are flesh and metaphor. Hollow pits where the graveworm burrows in, grows fat to sit and wait, transmuting all it sees into something rich and strange.

He licks his lips and smiles.

OH, YES, THIS ONE WILL SUFFICE. WELL DONE.

"Thank you master," Reverend White bows, turns to go.

BUT WHAT ABOUT YOUR REWARD?

"Ahh, thank you, my Lord. But, no, I—"

NO? YOU DARE REFUSE MY GIFT, MALAPENTH?

He makes noise, but no luck. Whimpers turn to screams as a blue light forms around his eyes, cracks spreading over the rippling white flesh that's ripped apart. I saw something at the heart of the thing that was no longer, or maybe never was, a man. Then it's gone: the light, the screams, and whatever Reverend White was.

All that is left is us. Us and the man with no eyes.

I don't know who you are. But if you've read this far I'm begging you: don't toss out these pages.; show someone... anyone.

He's heading west. There's something out there that he wants. He will kill to find it. He'll kill me, like he killed the others. But not before he's had his fun.

There is a war. I know that now, too late. We humans used to have names for the tumor-things that walk between the worlds. Those names are lost now or confused. For so long, we thought we were safe. But now I've seen it and I know we cannot hope to win. All we can do is prolong the end. But why did it have to be me?

I can feel him coming. There's no time. For God's sake, be quick.

Having left the US in 2018, Christopher Maleney has been travelling, working and honing the craft of writing. On farms and boats around Europe and the Americas, he has found connections, characters, and stories that deserve to be told. Pulling from the worlds of science fiction and fantasy, as well as the traditions of literature and poetry, his stories explore the variety of the human condition in its current and potential forms.

Find him on Twitter at @chris_maleney, and on Instagram as @strange_grotesques.

A Faun at Large:
A Garden State Saga

M.R. Blackmoor

Ces nymphes, je les veux perpétuer.

> —Stéphane Mallarmé, L'Après-Midi d'un Faune

I have lived with this horrendous virus for 47 years. After treatments with high strength CDS covering a period not exceeding 3 months overall, my genital herpes (HSV2) seemed to be completely cured. However, it is now over 18 months since my treatment, and the sores have returned. The boils are so painful.

> —Herpes-survivor Facebook posting

I

It was a mid-August Friday afternoon in Elizabeth and hotter than tickets to a Boss concert. The upright segment of the city's population had run for the shore, some going as far as Delaware to escape the heat and the local stench. Not that any of those fine folks would have been found in Dick's Filling Station, whose raunchiness was legendary even among Northern Jersey bars. Giovanni Caprese was a regular at Dick's and did not mind the hot weather, for he was always boiling inside with unspent energy and semi-processed jalapeño meat tacos, the house's specialty.

Very few people, except some family members, knew him as Giovanni. He was universally called Johnny *il Mela*, maybe because he drank mostly applejack; a half-drunk bottle of Laird's could often be seen on the table in front of him at Dick's. He explained his affinity for the liqueur (a blend of 35% apple brandy and 65% neutral spirits with a hint of apple flavor and aroma) by saying that as a teenager he worked one summer at a farm in Scobeyville in Monmouth County, where the drink was mainly produced, and became addicted to it. It didn't hurt that Applejack was relatively inexpensive. Moreover, Applejack was used to make a potent cocktail, a Jack Rose, which Johnny proffered to ladies whose already dubious virtue he sought to peg down another notch. In most cases, he got them under the table after the second cocktail, which they had carelessly ingested, misled by the drink's pretty pink color and innocent looking apple and cherry garnishes.

Johnny was a notorious lady's man, and his multiple conquests may have accounted also for his sobriquet—stories of his dalliances, usually initiated by him, often made the rounds at Dick's Filling Station and were repeated sardonically by the regulars.

There was still a third possible reason for Johnny Appleseed's nickname. A persistent story had it that he had contracted an incurable venereal disease from one of his early encounters with cheap Manhattan floozies, and now his penis uncontrollably dripped at most inopportune times. Had anyone dared question him directly on the matter, there would have been a volcanic eruption that put Mt. St. Helens to shame. But nobody did, aware as everyone was of his exceedingly bad temper. Johnny learned of the allegations only when a buxom waitress from Perth Amboy declined to bed with him for health reasons, which she proceeded to enumerate.

The rumor was, alas, true. Johnny had been suffering for a long time from abnormal discharges outside intercourse. These were thick and had a yellowish white tinge, with a ghastly odor that was hard to ignore. He had visited doctors who had ambiguously pointed to a variety of sexually transmitted diseases including chlamydia, gonorrhea, and mycoplasma as the potential culprits, but had been unable to specifically pinpoint the cause, let alone come up with a cure. A wide range of antibiotics had been prescribed and had proved ineffective.

What the doctors failed to recognize, but Johnny empirically observed, was that the only way to temporarily quell his symptoms was to pass on his affliction to another. He still remembered the incredulous expression on his urologist's face when he declared, "Doc, when I pop, it goes away, at least for a while." "No, Mr. Caprese," the physician had responded, "I'm afraid that's just a coincidence." But it was a coincidence that had played out quite a few times.

Therein lay the problem. Whatever the Molotov cocktail of sexually transmitted diseases that afflicted Johnny, he had developed some tolerance to the symptoms: constitutive soupy discharges, burning urine, painful sores, and constant itching. These were all annoyances with which Johnny could deal. On the other hand, his hapless paramours typically found Johnny's ministrations too much to bear. Rumor had it that some of the girls had even passed away within days of their trysts with Johnny. Even if these rumors were just that—tall tales recounted at seedy tanning parlors and hair salons—the word was out about Johnny: mess with the Caprese, and you'll get the horns. The local talent had heard enough to steer clear, and Johnny was in the midst of a grueling dry spell.

It was not in Johnny's nature to become despondent. A junior but promising member of an entrenched Jersey family, he faced challenges swiftly and often brutally, not letting conscience get in the way of results. But this dripping problem had him down, for he had been deprived of sex for almost four weeks. During this time, he had become one with his right hand. But solitary pleasures had become less fulfilling with each passing day. He needed human contact, soon.

With this thought burning on his mind like an open sore, Johnny sat at the bar at Dick's. The bartender, Tony, was tall and handsome and relatively salubrious for this part of Jersey. His main claim to fame was that he had bartended for six months at STK, in New York City's Meatpacking District. During his time there, he had roasted several desperate, yet well-to-do cougars, who lavished him with designer clothing and jewelry, and used him as an arm-piece while attending cheesy parties at hotels like the Tribeca Grand. So Tony was a bit more polished than the average Jersey boy.

As the old adage goes, however, you can take the kid out of Jersey, but you cannot take the Jersey out of the kid. Tony's stint at STK had come to a sudden end when his manager caught him raiding the cash register. Tony had stayed in Manhattan a bit longer, working as a waiter or bartender at various NYU college bars on Bleecker Street, but college students are stingier than wealthy society women, and before he knew it, Tony had found himself back in Jersey, working at Dick's Filling Station.

"Johnny, what's up, brother?" Tony said as he approached one of his most notorious customers. "What can I get you?" As he said this, he exchanged a firm high five with Johnny, clasping Caprese's hand.

"Hey chief," Johnny replied, "I'll have the usual."

"Coming right up. By the way, the rest of the gang is here, too."

While heading off to fix Johnny's Jack Rose, Tony gestured to four muscle-bound steak-jobs standing at the far end of the bar, wearing Ed Hardy shirts, tight jeans, and chains. They all had the same short, half-spikey haircut. One of them had frosted tips.

"Aw shit, is that Richie Catalano?" asked Johnny to himself, "I definitely need to have a drink first."

Tony returned with two drinks. "Who's the second drink for, man?" inquired Johnny.

"I thought I'd help you out, bro," replied Tony. "Three o'clock."

Johnny looked to his right, at a well-endowed, attractive yet trashy-looking hairdresser-type girl, bursting out of a Guns N' Roses tank top with a pair of daisy dukes and hooker heels. As she leaned over the bar to get Tony's attention, the back of her t-shirt rode up her back, revealing a faded tramp stamp. She was a true Jersey goddess.

"Who is that piece of ass?" asked Johnny.

"That, my friend, is for you to find out," said Tony, with a wink. "She started coming in here a few days ago. I'd be all over that myself, but she's friends with this girl I'm hooking up with, so I don't want to rock the boat. Knock yourself out."

"Thanks, bro," Johnny replied. "Real quick: which one of the two drinks is the PD?" ("PD" was their short for "panty dropper.") A little-known fact to which Johnny and few others were privy was that Tony once had been among Manhattan's most-heralded roofie-artists. He was a true MacGyver when it came to slipping a girl a mickey. With a couple Tylenol, some cough syrup, and few cubes of ice, Tony could concoct a potion that was equal parts aphrodisiac and sedative. The Bronx zoo was said to have called on Tony to help when Quang-Xi, a female panda, had repeatedly rebuffed the advances of her presumptive mate, a feisty male panda called General Tso. It had worked, and the new panda cub was already being scheduled for return to the mother country.

Despite enjoying the mild suspense of watching Johnny down a girl with a series of Jack Roses, Tony occasionally felt charitable enough to eliminate chance altogether and assist Johnny with a PD.

Tony looked tellingly at one of the drinks. Johnny nodded in acknowledgement, licked the index and pinky fingers of his right hand, ran them through his eyebrows, and was off to the races.

With all the charm he could muster, Johnny leaned over. "Hey, gorgeous. What's your name?"

"Are you talking to me?" replied the Jersey princess frostily.

"Yeah. What's your name?"

"Angela."

"Angela... are you an angel?"

"Yeah, I guess," responded Angela. If one looked closely, one might have seen at that moment an incipient blush fighting its way to the surface of her tan.

"Well, Angela. Let me tell you a secret," Johnny said as he leaned in. "I've never seen an angel with a pair of knockers like yours before."

Angela laughed, "Oh my Gawd, you're gonna get us hit by lightning! I bet you've never seen an angel before."

"No, trust me. I'd know. I've been to all the churches. Even St. Anthony's over in Paramus, overlooking the Turnpike."

"Oh stop! And what's *your* name?"

"I'm Johnny."

"Nice to meet you, Johnny."

"Pleasure is all mine, Angela darling. Here, I got this drink for you. Take a sip." Johnny offered her the PD.

"Oh thanks! What is it?"

"Why don't you take a sip and guess?"

Angela sipped the glass and began pondering. One could practically hear the hamster wheel in her head begin to turn.

"How do you like your drink?" As Angela took another sip, Johnny gently pushed the bottom of her glass, indicating that she should drink more. The two began making chit-chat for a few minutes. They talked about what it was like to grow up in Jersey, the rest stops, Bon Jovi, and Bill Parcells.

"So, Angela," he finally said, "do you wanna get out of here?"

Angela wanted to tell him, "no." But she couldn't. The PD was already starting to take effect. Without knowing what she was doing, she said "yes." The following day, she wouldn't really know where they went after Dick's Filling Station. Visually it was all a blur, and all she could hear was a cacophony of Def Leppard and Johnny rambling about the one time he had run into Bill Belichick at a gas station on the Garden State parkway and how much she'd love the autographed Chris Candido poster on his bedroom wall. Angela was powerless to comment on any of this. She did, however, note that her clothes reeked of a lingering feral odor.

Angela was pronounced dead a week later in the Emergency Room of the Jersey Shore Medical Center in Hackensack. The cause of death was unknown. But one internist likened the scar tissue built up around her private parts to a case of leprosy he had once witnessed while volunteering for the Peace Corps in Papua, New Guinea. Her parents were despondent. Not only was their daughter dead, but news of the tragedy had reached them just hours before they were supposed to attend a Springsteen concert. They ended up selling their lawn seats on Craigslist for $17.99 each, almost half their face value. It was a terrible afternoon for them, perhaps the most trying one of their lives.

II

The news of Angela's demise eventually reached Johnny's ears. As he sat another steamy afternoon at his usual table at the Filling Station, Johnny pondered what to do. He suspected that his venereal diseases proved fatal to the women with whom he had commerce. This was not a problem he could discuss with his buddies at Dick's or with other family members. After a while, he concluded that there was only one person in whom Johnny could confide: his grandfather Vito Caprese, the head of the Caprese clan, still alive and spending his final days in a retirement home in Edison.

To anyone else in Johnny's immediate family, the notion of a counseling session with grandpa Vito would have been ludicrous. Vito had convinced them years before that he had lost the faculty of speech and that fate had relegated him to a quasi-vegetative existence. For years, Johnny, too, had lived under this impression.

It all changed for Johnny around the time he had reached puberty. On one summer day in 1990, Johnny was alone in the living room with Vito and his high school yearbook, while the second half of a Yankees doubleheader played on the television. With Vito sitting listlessly in his wheelchair and no one else in the house, Johnny thought the moment opportune to squeeze out some "gentleman's relish" while admiring a photograph of ninth grade heartthrob Tina Cuccinello. Just as things were getting good, Johnny leapt from his seat at the sound of words—actual words—emanating from Vito's mouth, "Don't fuck around, kid. Give it to her... goooooood!" Johnny proceeded to cringe, both at his own shame and at the sight of his grandfather following up his utterance, perhaps his first in years, with an attempt to lick his own cheeks lustily. To this day, Johnny had etched in his mind's eye the image of his grandfather's corroded, sore-riddled tongue, which very much resembled the outer skin of a beaded lizard. Frighteningly, Vito had almost succeeded in licking his cheeks.

From then on, Vito took Johnny under his wing and, during their private moments, instructed him in the arts of seduction, Jersey-style. Vito also warned Johnny many times that, if he did not have sex early and often, fate would punish him with unspeakable maladies that would burn him down low, where it counted. Johnny often thought of Vito's admonishments whenever his symptoms flared up.

Johnny decided he needed counsel from his *nonno*. He hopped into his favorite girl, Brenda, a restored 1966 flaming red 289 V8 Mustang convertible, and got onto Route 9, speakers blasting Human Remains' *Rote* —one of the defunct band's most enduring tunes. He had plunked his entire share of the first job he ran for the family to buy Brenda, but it was worth all the money he had to be able to zoom down the Turnpike at way above the speed limit, wind mussing his hair, inflicting heavy metal blasts on the cars he passed.

It was only a half an hour drive down to Edison, but Johnny fretted all the way there. After all, Johnny hated guilt trips, and he had the undeniable feeling that he was in for one, given that his constant hunt for fresh tail, not to mention his overall indolence, had prevented him from visiting his *nonno* in several years. Making matters worse, the onset of dementia had exacerbated Vito's cantankerous traits, which was not difficult to do, given that Vito was, at core, a grouchy curmudgeon, a characteristic brought about by years of hard living. The older Caprese was fond of recounting reminiscences of his early years in the *Sassi di Matera,* which according to his tales was one of the worst dumps on Earth. He always made it clear that

Matera was in Basilicata, at the heel of the Italian peninsula, and was nowhere near the cesspool that was Sicily (as with their cousins in the states, Italians living in the old country can be a territorial lot).

Johnny always thought that the disclaimer was funny, for upon arrival in America in 1949 Vito Caprese had settled in Elizabeth and gone to work as a janitor and sanitation worker at a landfill owned by the Badami crime family. A Sicilian family, the Badamis had purchased the landfill so they could more easily dispose of unwanted contraband and the remains of their victims. For the most part, they and their henchmen looked down on Vito, mainly because of his Materan ancestry. If they ever visited the men's room in the landfill operator's office while he was mopping, they would make a point to piss on the floor, so they could watch him clean it up, which he would have no choice but to do, often while cursing under his breath. One time, one of the mobsters had even masturbated to completion in front of Vito, as well as some of his buddies, whom he had tried to impress by claiming that he could shoot across a room (as it turned out, he could make it to Vito's shoes). But it was precisely because of Vito's unassuming nature and appearance that various Badami capo regimes occasionally used Vito to mule for them. Indeed, Vito had made a decent supplemental income running low-grade narcotics, like Quaaludes and molly, for the Sicilians. In this way, he had managed to provide a reasonable middle-class life for his children and grandchildren.

After revealing his still functional powers of speech to Johnny, Vito had made sure that his favorite grandson realized the importance of supplemental income and linked up with connected Sicilianos of his own generation who occasionally need Materan help in moving a few grams here and there. Selling cheap club drugs was how Johnny managed to pay for his membership at Gold's Gym and numerous tanning bills.

Indeed, Johnny was full of memories as he sought to shave a few minutes off his commute by winding through Edison's suburban backstreets in route to the Evergreen Gardens nursing home, to which Vito Caprese had been moved by his sons, including Johnny's father, when he began giving incipient signs of psychotic behavior. They had essentially left him there to die, and besides paying the nursing home bills, paid no attention to him or to the medical staff, which occasionally tried to contact them regarding his health.

Evergreen Gardens was a small facility on a quiet street not far from the Garden State Parkway. From the outside, it looked just like many other low-rise nursing homes dotted across America. Evergreen's common areas sported Early American furniture and overstuffed sofas and armchairs covered with washable fabrics in large prints. The resident rooms had single beds, minimal accessories, and Kinkade prints on the walls. The place was clean but devoid of character, and was reminiscent of a discount motel.

Johnny found Vito in his room arguing with an attendant. "Mr. Caprese, you *must* take your medication. You know you get restless if you miss even one dose." The beefy nurse sounded weary but resigned.

"Bullshit, you stinking whore!" was the shouted response of the scrawny man on the wheelchair. "I don't need no pills. You are just trying to poison me."

"Mr. Caprese, I am not a 'stinking whore,' and this is antipsychotic medication, it is very important you take it."

"No way. Shove it up your loose cunt."

"Mr. Caprese! Watch your mouth!"

"Why don't you watch it, instead!" Vito squinted his eyes and began rapidly flicking his tongue up and down, in mock cunnilingus.

At this point, Johnny interjected himself into the conversation. "*Ciao, nono. Come sta?*"

The old man turned away from the nurse and faced Johnny with an expression of disbelief. "Giovanni, *sei tu?*"

"*Si, papo. Son'io.*"

As the senior Caprese stared at his grandson, the nurse turned toward Johnny with a sense of relief. "Are you his grandson?" she asked.

Johnny replied that he was. She responded, "Well, I'll leave the two of you alone. He's in quite a mood today. Maybe you can convince him to take these."

The nurse handed the pills to Johnny as she walked out the room. On her way out, Vito tried unsuccessfully to grope her breasts. Johnny stared briefly at the pills and then tossed them into the waste basket in the corner of the room.

Vito's face turned to suspicion. "What do you want? You have not come visit me in almost five years. Are you in trouble? Are you having money problems?"

"No, papo. I have enough."

"Then, what is it?"

"You see..." Johnny hesitated, gulped, and went on to describe his difficulty as briefly as he could, turning crimson in the process.

"Ah, that," was Vito's laconic response.

"You don't seem surprised. You always said it would happen if I didn't fuck enough."

Vito shrugged. "I believe it runs in the family, but sometimes it skips a generation or two."

"What do you mean?" asked Johnny, astonished.

Vito closed his eyes for a moment and his face drained of expression, as if he was drifting away. Finally, he came to and replied in a voice that had a different intonation and sounded much younger than his eighty seven years: "Did I ever tell you how we came to change our family name?"

"What change? Weren't we always the Caprese clan?"

"No, no, no. When I was born, our family in the Sassi was known as the Agnelli. But as I got into my teens, this need to screw we have been talking about started cropping up. At the age of thirteen, I was already getting *la mia minchia* in every hole I could find, which at the time meant farm animals. Finally, as grew older, I switched my attention to the young girls in the village... and the family."

"But how did your parents put up with your behavior?"

"My father was somewhat tolerant of my indiscretions because he felt, with pride, that they were the result of my being very male, *di avere i grandi coglioni.*" But, when I was seventeen, I was caught by Aunt Lola violating her nine-year old daughter, something that the family could not forgive. I was kicked out of our hovel in Sassi and after tumbling all over Basilicata made the jump to Sicilia. It was in Sicilia that I first felt the scourge on my sausage after a dalliance with this village girl named Apollonia. I went to the village doctor, who told me that, from his experience with other patients, the disease was like a hot potato and that the only way to get rid of it was to pass it on to a hooker or barnyard animal. So that's what I tried to do, for years, and with anything I could get my hands on. After a while, the villagers got used to the sight of me helping myself to their livestock, particularly goats, which were everywhere back then. So, they began calling me Caprese, and since the Agnellis had disowned me, 'Caprese' was the name I gave the immigration officers at Ellis Island when I made the jump to this country as a stowaway on a ship full of immigrants."

"And you never tried to find a permanent cure when you were in America?"

"Not really. I was quite satisfied with the folk remedy that the Siciliano doctor had prescribed. Chasing tail was not anything that bothered me, *ma* it drove your *nonna* insane. She made me go to a shrink, who said I suffered from satyriasis and prescribed tranquilizers and herbal teas to calm me down. They never did anything." Vito's voice trailed off as he momentarily lost himself in thought before resuming, "The strange thing is that your grandmother was somehow immune to the symptoms of the affliction, although other girls and animals were not."

"So, *caro papo, che devo fare?* What should I do about my problem?"

"*Figlio mio*, you have two problems. You have to find a cure for your *male di cazzo*, those diseases that keep you dripping like a leaky faucet. But the other thing, the need to always be in the hunt for pussy, has no cure and will be with you until you cannot get it up, and even after then."

"Managgia, nonno. I'm screwed."

"Ma perchè?"

"Because the doctors don't know how to get rid of whatever is making me leaky."

"Well, in that case...." Vito seemed to ponder for a moment. "You will need to keep trying to find fresh pussy."

As he drove back from Edison, Johnny could not shake the haunting image of his grandfather perfecting his power stroke by making his way through herds of sheep and she-goats in the old country. In any event, it amazed Johnny how vastly different his grandfather turned out to be from the man he had seen at family-get togethers during much of his childhood: mute, frozen, and half-comatose, but somewhat dignified while parked in a rusty wheelchair at the head of the dinner table. Would that be Johnny one day?

III

WWNJ was the most popular TV station in Northern Jersey. While affiliated with Fox, the station carried independent programming, largely to the taste of its target audience. A trademark of WWNJ was its inclination to deploy buxom girls as part of its local news team. The sight of scantily clad reporters prancing about the studio or on location at the site of the latest bank robbery or drug bust brought some of the most excitable male viewers over the edge with messy consequences.

Perhaps the most famous mare in the WWNJ stable was Blanca O'Reilly, a stunning half-caste with green eyes, caramel skin and boobs that triggered burglar alarms when they bumped into doors. Blanca was actually an accomplished reporter, who could conduct a mean interview by shaking her maracas to loosen the lips of otherwise circumspect witnesses. Her specialty, developed over several years with the network, was to track the coming and goings of the leading families in the Garden State. It was the admissions during her interview of a minor *capo* that led to the third conviction of Angelo Prisco, one of the most notorious members of the Genovese family. Blanca was appreciated and lusted after by most of her viewers.

It was that reporting zeal that drew Blanca to Dick's Filling Station one unseasonably hot Wednesday afternoon in mid-September. She was trying to track down a lead on a crime ring responsible for distributing petty club drugs, as well as laced scratch-and-sniff stickers, in the Greater New York area. Johnny's name had come up in conversation with one of her contacts. After a lot of digging, she located his hangout in an Elizabeth bar and decided to pay him a visit.

Tony was standing behind the bar, pretending to be busy cleaning beer glasses even though the joint was almost deserted. As Blanca strutted in and stood in front of the bar, Tony—who had failed to recognize her at first—did a double take and greeted her effusively: "Why, Miss O'Reilly! Honored to meet you in person! I am a great fan, you know! Can I offer you anything?"

Blanca, who was used to the adoration of her fans, gave a tiny smile and replied almost curtly: "Diet Coke, please."

Tony busied himself filling a glass with ice and pouring a soft drink. As he handed it to Blanca he asked: "What brings you to our modest establishment?"

"I'm looking for someone called Johnny Caprese. Do you know him?"

"No shit. Oh, pardon my French! Yes, I know him well. He comes here often."

"Do you expect him any time soon?"

"He usually does not come on Thursdays, but I expect he'll be here tomorrow afternoon about this time."

"I will return then. Thanks for the information." She slurped the rest of the Coke and got up to leave. "How much do I owe you?"

"Nothing, Miss O'Reilly. It's on the house. See you tomorrow?"

"I think so. Thank you for the drink and the information."

"My pleasure."

As Blanca exited the bar, Tony picked up his cell phone. "Yo, Johnny, this is Tony. How's it hanging?" ... "Yeah, fine. Same shit. Listen, you had a visitor today." ... "A very nice visitor." ... "Yeah, do you know Blanca O'Reilly of WWNJ?" ... "She came looking for you." ... "No, I'm not shitting you. I told her you would be here tomorrow afternoon and she is coming back to meet you." ... "No, I don't know what she wants, but she's a real piece, so you better put on your best duds." ... "Same to you, motherfucker. Bye."

Johnny's vanity was stroked by the news. He immediately made an appointment to have his eyebrows tweezed. However, on his way back from the salon he became apprehensive because everyone in Jersey knew the Prisco story. He decided to be very careful when he met the journalist.

Friday afternoon the Filling Station was even more deserted than the day before. Indeed, when Blanca arrived—dressed to the nines—only Tony was at the place. "Has Mr. Caprese shown up yet?" she immediately asked.

"No, but he called earlier, and I expect him momentarily. Can I get you another Diet Coke, or maybe something else?"

"No, thanks. I had a late lunch."

"Why don't you sit down and wait for him? It won't be long."

"Thanks." She had barely sat down when the door swung open and Johnny, wearing his newest pair of Diesel jeans and a shiny gray short-sleeved muscle shirt, ambled in as if he owned the whole wide world, subtly flexing to impress her with his muscle tone. Tony rushed to make the introductions. "Hello, Johnny. Please meet Miss Blanca O'Reilly, who is here to see you."

Johnny put on his most charming smile and proffered his hand in welcome. "*Enchanté*" he crooned (actually pronouncing the word "An-Chan-tea"). "De-elighted to meet you. I gotta say you are even more beautiful in person than on TV."

Blanca responded with a wry smile that failed to warm her face. "Pleased to meet you."

"Is this a social call, darling? If it is, I would invite you to join me in a more private place so we can get better acquainted."

"Unfortunately, I'm here on business. I understand you worked for Mr. Francesco Guarraci and we are researching to do a piece on him as a leading citizen of the North Jersey community. Perhaps you could help me with some questions about him and his business activities, on which I'm sure you can shed some light."

Johnny frowned, but quickly smoothed his features into a look of polite interest. "Sure, just let me know what you want to know. But, will you join me for a little drink?"

"Sorry, I don't drink while I'm on the job."

"That's honorable and all, but this is a special cocktail that Tony here invented. Can we ask him to fix us a couple?"

"Again, I don't drink while I'm on business."

"Listen, doll, I tell you what: I'll ask Tony to bring us a glass so you can see what we're talking about." Before she could protest again, Johnny turned to Tony, who had pretended to be oblivious to the conversation but had not missed a word. "Tony, could you hook us up with a couple of Jack Roses, and please use the fancy glasses that you keep hidden under the counter?"

"Sure, boss" was Tony's unctuous reply.

Blanca wasted no time getting on with the interview. "How long have you worked for Mr. Guarraci?"

"Oh, let me think... It's a little over six years."

"And what do you do for his company?"

"I do a number of things, but I am mainly responsible for accounts receivable, you know invoicing, collections, things like that." The conversation stopped when Tony approached with two liqueur glasses filled to the rim with a lovely pink liquid. He placed one in front of Blanca and the other before Johnny.

"Hey, wouldn't it be cool if we sipped them at the same time?" implored Johnny.

Blanca relented. "Well, just a sip. I'm not much of a drinker." She brought the small glass to her lips and inhaled the aroma. "Smells like apple blossoms, but somehow sweeter," she declared.

"Damn right, give it a taste." Blanca swirled a small amount inside her mouth, admiring the complex flavor and the rich bouquet of the concoction. "It's delicious," she reluctantly admitted.

"Have some more" urged Johnny. "The taste grows on you."

She swallowed one small gulp, then took a larger one. Johnny leaned in closely, studying her features intently and starting to get hard. Blanca noticed, for the first time, a musky odor emanating from Johnny, which was probably his having doused himself with Aqua Velva. "I like it," she said.

"But let's continue. What kinds of receivables are those that you collect for Mr. Guarraci?"

"Well, as you know, his main line of business is in farm equipment. I deal with small farmers in Southern Jersey and collect on their purchases of tractors, combines, and other such devices."

"And... what..." Blanca paused as if losing her train of thought. "I mean, what...?"

She never finished the sentence. The empty glass fell from her hand and Johnny had to move quickly to catch her before she fell out of her chair.

Tuesday afternoon, Chet Jobs, Blanca's news anchor at WWNJ, had a solemn message for the viewership to start off the 6 O'Clock News: "We begin tonight's show with a sad story. We regret to inform you that Blanca O'Reilly passed away earlier today after checking herself in at the Jersey Shore Medical Center. Medical staff and authorities are still investigating the precise cause of death, and WWNJ will keep you posted."

IV

At age forty-three, Giovanna Balducci was the epitome of unfulfilled potential. Born to a wealthy socialite couple in Milan, Italy, Giovanna combined natural beauty with an alert mind that had gained her a first-rate education. After obtaining a law degree from the *Universita degli Studi di Roma La Sapienza* and an L.L.M. from Columbia University, she had joined a major Milanese firm and settled into a comfortable legal practice as a litigator. She generally enjoyed the work environment, which she spiced up every now and then with a work-place affair.

Despite her professional triumphs, Giovanna suffered from a mounting sense of ennui. She was an outlier in Italian society, not only because of her family's wealth and her superlative education, but also due to her anomalous romantic life. Giovanna had never married, and either sought out married men, whom she knew to be unavailable from the outset, or, if she found herself in a reasonably healthy relationship, she would cheat on her boyfriend; by playing the betrayer, she protected herself from making any commitments. This sort of free-booting lifestyle had served her well through her twenties and early thirties, but, with age, Giovanna's looks had begun to fade, and between her deteriorating physique, hostility toward men, and the long hours she usually logged at the office, she saw her prospects of settling down dwindle.

Suddenly, her career also took a hit. In 2012, her firm landed one of the highest profile court cases in Italy. It involved a raunchy Pringles potato chips commercial, in which acclaimed Italian adult film actor Rocco Siffredi boasted about how he preferred Pringles to all the other "potato chips" that he'd ever tasted. The claim involved a risqué play on words, as *patata* is both the Italian conventional word for "potato" and a slang name for "pussy." Although the Pringles ad was a hit with the younger generation, many citizens found it appalling and prevailed upon the Ministry of Communication to ban it. This led to widespread protests, and Rocco Siffredi became an icon and rallying figure for freedom-loving Italians wary of government censorship. Giovanna's assignment to Siffredi's freedom of speech suit by the head of her firm's litigation department was to boost her resume in the push to make her a partner.

Unfortunately for Pringles, Siffredi, and Giovanna, the assignment came at a time when Giovanna's negative feelings towards men were at their nadir. Unable to stomach serving as the zealous advocate for Siffredi, whose misogynistic, street style of porn was as sinister to girls as it was popular among adolescent males around the world, Giovanna tanked the case. Giovanna botched routine depositions, wrote incoherent motions, and missed filing deadlines, leading to the case's dismissal.

In a normal work environment, Giovanna would have lost her job. However, she had bedded several members of the firm's board, and fearing that she might spill the beans to their spouses, they kept her around, although they slowly weaned her off meaningful matters, effectively hamstringing her career.

Somehow, her story was luridly captured by a tabloid that paraded her incompetence and referred to her as the *"sterile principessa"* and depicted her life as that of a shameless and convention-defying bachelorette.

Despite her swelling antipathy toward men, Giovanna did, in fact, yearn for a child. Throughout her travails, she visited her gynecologist frequently and was always popping hormone pills and other supplements to ensure maximum fertility. The problem was that she had now become a notorious man-eater and no males in her social and professional circles would chance getting involve with her.

So, Giovanna decided to take a vacation in the States and search among her former Columbia classmates for a willing sperm supplier. After arriving in New York, Giovanna spent a week serially dating her former classmates. It was all very much disheartening, because not one of them sought to invite her for a nightcap. Some simply were not interested in anything more than a drink; others just could not read between the lines and comprehend the obvious signs of interest that she tried to give off. And her faded beauty provided no incentives for the guys to walk into the trap.

Having given up her attempts to lure nerdy intellectuals into her bed, Giovanna decided to spend the last two days of her trip visiting with an old female friend from her LLM days. Her friend had a lucrative immigration practice in Elizabeth, New Jersey, and Giovanna looked forward to spending some time away from men. It all went well, but on the last night of her stay she found herself alone in town, since her friend had another engagement.

Giovanna had a simple but satisfying meal at a local Italian diner and consumed a whole bottle of Chianti by herself. Feeling a bit woozy, Giovanna went for a stroll along the sidewalks of the downtown area to clear her mind. She eventually felt the need to respond to a call of nature and went into a dive called "Dick's Filling Station." Giovanna entered the establishment, waited in the line to the lady's room for what seemed like an eternity, and finally relieved herself.

While exiting the bar, she chanced upon a scuffle between two testosterone-laden men. The dispute apparently arose when the more aggressive of the men had stormed out of the establishment with his head down and accidentally bumped into the other guy. There ensued the standard exchange of pleasantries regarding one another's mothers, followed by some pushing, and then the grabbing and yanking of necklaces. A bouncer moved in before things could really heat up. Giovanna noticed that the more aggressive of the two meatheads, who apparently knew and was friendly with the bouncer, kept baring his teeth and pulling up his muscle shirt to show off his abs once it became obvious that no fight would ensue.

Satisfied that he had given off the impression of having cowed his opponent into docility, the brute turned to leave, when out of the corner of his eye he caught a glimpse of Giovanna. He nonchalantly moseyed over toward her. "I'm sorry you had to see that, darling," he apologized. Giovanna responded that it was no big deal and that every man must stand up for himself. She was strangely turned on by his bellicosity, which was a welcome change from the craven and unmanly lawyers she encountered on both sides of the pond. Observing her pure, if alcohol-slurred Northern Italian accent, the almost-street fighter remarked, "So, you're from the old country? What's your name?"

"Giovanna... and yes, I am from *Italia*. What is your name and where are you from?"

"*Che coincidenza! Inoltre mi chiamo Giovanni, come lei*," he said with a toothy smile. "*Sono di cui, di Jersey.*" Can I buy you a wonderful cocktail that is the *specialità di queste bar?*

A bit later, Giovanna found herself waking up lying naked on her back in Johnny's bed. Johnny, also naked, stood over her. As Johnny ejaculated inside her, she was convinced that her egg had been fertilized. She crooned, "I feel the life, it grows inside of me."

Giovanna did not bother spending the night. Johnny had fallen asleep within minutes of finishing, and Giovanna quickly dressed and left. On her way out, she noticed that the room smelled something like a barn.

It took only three hours for Giovanna to realize that something was wrong. She felt a sharp pang in the inside of her womb. At first, she thought it was from her fertilized egg implanting, so she smiled to herself and went to sleep. A few hours later, the pain became unbearable. She awoke in her plush hotel room in Manhattan in a cold sweat, her private parts figuratively on fire with a searing, burning itch. She resisted scratching for a while, but before long found herself clawing frenziedly at the inside of her vagina with both hands. From the blood on her fingers she knew that she had ruptured a blood vessel. She began bleeding profusely, so she ran to the bathroom of the hotel looking for her toiletry bag to see if she might stop the bleeding with a tampon. When she found that she had run out of supplies, she rushed back into the main room to call the front desk. The half-asleep clerk could barely understand her, but promised to call 9-1-1. Meanwhile, the pain intensified. Giovanna screamed in agony and rushed back into the bathroom, planning to sit on the toilet and bleed into toilet. She was concerned that she might lose her child. Her mind was so pre-occupied with this thought, as well as her pain, that she forgot to side step the large puddle of blood beside the sink. She slipped on the wet surface and smashed the back of her head against the sink, splitting her skull wide open. When the paramedics arrived, Giovanna was delusional due to the loss of blood. She thought that she was in the delivery room. One young female paramedic caught a glimpse of Giovanna's exposed crotch and screamed in terror. Summoning every last ounce of strength left in her, Giovanna asked, "Nurse, is it a boy or a girl?"

Giovanna died without hearing the answer.

V

Unlike his other victims, Giovanna came from an affluent and well-connected family. Her father, a famous art dealer, made a big fuss over her death with the Italian politicians who in turn began pestering the State Department so that, at the end, both the FBI and the Center for Disease Control in Atlanta were brought in to investigate Giovanna's mysterious death, which the coroner had attributed to a previously unclassified strain or combination of strains of deadly venereal diseases. The CDC dispatched Clarisse Schmidt, an ambitious young epidemiologist and health specialist, to Northern New Jersey to look into Giovanna's death and those of several other women who had died under similar circumstances.

Clarisse, a born detective, found in Giovanna's purse the receipt from the diner where she had her last meal on earth, and armed with a picture of Giovanna, started walking the streets of Elizabeth looking for someone who could identify her. As luck would have it, Clarisse ran into the bouncer at Dick's Filling Station who recalled having seen her having a couple of drinks and leaving the bar in the company of Johnny Caprese.

When the Feds (accompanied by NJ State Troopers and Clarisse) invaded The Filling Station and roughed up Tony a bit, they learned additional details on the story of Giovanna's meeting with the young Mr. Caprese, her sudden indisposition, and Johnny's gallant endeavor to drive her to her home.

A few days later, law enforcement agents showed up at Antonio Guarraci's headquarters and proceeded to arrest Johnny, charging him with the suspected murder of Giovanna.

VI

Johnny's apprehension by the FBI and the New Jersey authorities was not the end of the story, but a mere beginning to the sensational events that followed. The case against Johnny was built by the discovery of faint vomit stains on Brenda's passenger seat, which the lab reported matched Giovanna's DNA. Small samples of her DNA were also found at various points of Johnny's apartment, including notably the top of a dinette table.

A critical discovery was that of a crumpled facial tissue between the cushions of the living room of Johnny's apartment. The tissue contained a bit of dried blood and a substance that was identified as semen. The provenance of the semen became a crucial clue in the investigation, and the Union County Prosecutor in charge of the case got the County's Superior Court to order that a sample of Johnny's DNA be obtained and matched against that of the semen found in the tissue.

When Johnny's DNA was analyzed, a startling discovery was made. In addition to the twenty-three pairs of chromosomes found in every human's cell, Johnny had two extra pairs of strange chromosomes whose structure was unlike anything specialists had ever seen. After a lot of referrals to other specialists, an animal geneticist working for a livestock company in Australia reported that the strange chromosomes were analogous to those found in goats, but appeared more primitive, as if it belonged to some ancestor of today's goat (*Capra aegagrus hircus*), and the wild goats of Eastern Europe.

Based on Giovanna's peculiar symptoms, investigators were able to link Johnny to several gruesome deaths of women in the Greater New York area, including Blanca. Given the scope of the case and the various jurisdictions involved, Johnny's prosecution was transferred to the United States District Court for the Southern District of New York, sitting in Manhattan.

It did not take long for the story to leak out and receive attention both by legitimate publications like *Nature*, and earthier ones. A spread in the *New York Post* dubbed Johnny "a satyr" and described him as a serial rapist, "in keeping with his mythological roots as an insatiable pursuer of female flesh."

The lawyer representing Johnny, Carlo Ragano, was personally selected by the Guarraci family's underboss Joe Miranda because he excelled in the ability to confuse juries into acquitting even hardened criminals. At Johnny's arraignment, Ragano instructed him to plead "not guilty" to the murder of Giovanna and seven other women, and requested a bench conference in which he advised the trial judge and the District Attorney that he intended to argue at trial, if there was one, that any deaths that Johnny may have caused were the result of his peculiar genetic makeup, citing the controversial *Durham v. United States* case in which a New Hampshire court had ruled that a defendant is entitled to acquittal if his crime was the product of his illness. Ragano argued that "as the papers eloquently describe it, Mister Caprese is a latter-day faun, and a faun cannot be blamed or punished for behaving like one—assiduously pursuing nymphs or, in this modern age, young women. In addition, these women were not murdered. They somehow died as a result of having intercourse with my client." The judge was skeptical and the District Attorney's lawyer apoplectic, but the judge allowed the not guilty plea to be entered on Johnny's behalf.

The period leading to the trial was rife with colorful media stories and raunchy "exposés." Late night TV comedians made "the New Jersey faun" the subject of one-liners, off-color skits, and fake interviews. Johnny Caprese became a household word and a synonym for lechery but, on the advice of Ragano, stayed silent through all of this. And, in an Edison nursing home, Vito Caprese now spent his days hunting down articles about his *caro nipote* Giovanni and pasting them in a new scrapbook. He was bursting with pride.

VI

The trial was a legal landmark and a media circus. Many articles in learned psychology and ethics journals were written exploring the issues of freedom of will and personal responsibility. Can a man be held accountable for acts over which he has little or no control? Should a man be convicted if he has awareness of his acts and their likely consequences and undertakes them nonetheless? Is the existence of an overwhelming animal imperative enough to override one's duty to abstain? Many argued that these were bogus issues, and Johnny should be found guilty and given a long prison sentence. Others argued for confinement to a mental health institution, or even acquittal.

The trial developed across predictable lines. The prosecution brought up Johnny's mafia ties, his nefarious activities as a *capo* of the Guarraci family, and his deliberate efforts to cover his tracks after each life ending liaison. It argued that, in the case of Blanca, Johnny's failed attempts to remove all traces of her presence in his apartment were conclusive proof that the defendant had tried to remove any evidence that she had been on the premises with him. "Those are not the acts of an insane man, but the tactics of a methodical assassin." As for fatally infecting the other women, the prosecution quoted the long-standing "depraved heart" rule whereby a person is guilty of second-degree murder if he deliberately perpetrates a knowingly dangerous act with reckless and wanton unconcern as to whether another person is harmed. "There is no doubt that Mr. Caprese's heart is as depraved and malignant as one can find."

Most of the witnesses called by Ragano were experts. One, a famous pathologist who had performed post-mortem examination of the bodies of the women linked to Johnny, and indicated that their deaths were probably caused by the same potent mix of pathogens that were present in Johnny's body and that caused his symptoms, and which were "at best as it could be determined" due to his animal condition. "Perhaps the fauns of legend sought intercourse as the palliative for their own physical woes. Indeed, that was the situation with Mr. Caprese."

Another expert witness called by Ragano was a noted psychologist. He declared under oath that Johnny was the victim of irresistible impulses from his animal brain and he no more could have exercised control over his behavior than an owl could have ceased pursuing mice. "Mr. Caprese is what he is—a living anachronism, a man with the urges of an ancient, non-human creature. He should be acquitted, as he is not responsible for his actions."

The trial lasted almost two weeks and, at the end of it, the jury deliberated for another one. When they emerged, they declared themselves to be hung. They could not agree on any verdict, whether it resulted in Johnny's exoneration, commitment to a mental institution, or imprisonment.

When the non-verdict was announced, the presiding judge thanked and dismissed the jury and summoned counsel to his chambers. He minced no words in expressing his dismay at the situation. "In my estimation, another trial might well be futile. I invite both sides to come up with a compromise that satisfies the needs of justice and the interests of the public."

Ragano had been thinking about this for some time, and responded: "Your Honor, I recognize that we all see the need to get my client out of circulation. Neither he nor I would agree to a solution that involves confinement in a prison or a mental institution. But perhaps it would be possible to have him sent to some sort of place of retirement."

"Do you have anything specific in mind?" retorted the judge.

"Yes, your Honor, I have been making discrete inquiries and there is a Meditation Center in a remote location in Idaho that would agree to host him if a suitable donation is made on his behalf. I have spoken to Mr. Guarraci and he is willing, even eager, to defray the costs involved in Mr. Caprese's relocation away from New Jersey so that his company's reputation is no longer tainted by this scandal."

"Is Mr. Caprese willing to go?"

"I expect he can be persuaded."

"What is the position of the Government?"

"We feel that another trial could result in justice being meted out, but might again lead to further public dissension and discontent. I will of course need to consult my superiors but I expect we would all be happy to see this one go away."

"Well, I will draft an order dismissing the case with prejudice, but will not release it until you have submitted an acceptable settlement agreement between all parties. Please prepare one at your earliest convenience." In the meantime, Mr. Caprese is to remain under house arrest.

"Thank you, your Honor."

"And, Mr. Ragano, make sure that the agreement stipulates that in selecting a center in which to place Mr. Caprese, provisions are made to keep him away from boys and females of all ages. That will be all."

Sadly, the Meditation Center was not able to host its notorious guest for very long. Johnny Caprese disappeared, leaving behind a score of dead nuns whose cadavers exhibited gruesome symptoms. Johnny became an urban legend all over the Pacific Northwest.

At about the same time, Vito Caprese ran away from his retirement home. Reports of his having been spotted in farms as far as Connecticut were never confirmed.

M.R. Blackmoor is the pen name of two US-based writers: Matias F. Travieso-Diaz and his co-author on this story, a Washington DC attorney. Mr. Travieso-Diaz is a Cuban-American engineer and attorney, retired after half a century of professional practice. Following retirement, he has taken up creative writing and authored many short stories of various genres. His stories have appeared or are scheduled to appear in over two dozen paying publications in the United States, the U.K., Canada, Australia and New Zealand. Mr. Travieso-Diaz's co-author is a prominent attorney still in private practice, who has publications in the fields of law and history.

No Mama, No Papa

Jonathan Titchenal

We were filthy, and we were lousy, and we stank, and he loved us.

So he said.

MacArthur loved a lot of things and people when they were useful to him. We were useful to him. Not for killing-the-Nips reasons, but because his love for us made good PR.

MacArthur loved us because MacArthur loved MacArthur. Wrap your head around that one.

I was having a moderately paranoid episode the day the big guy in the aviator sunglasses decided to stop by Bataan to tell us how great we all were. This was a man who could stare, mirrorshades reflecting your wasting frame, into the faces of the men he was responsible for torturing slowly to death, and tell them he loved them. And mean it.

Humans. Ain't we something.

This was all before, you understand. Or maybe it's still happening, somewhere. I was just a grunt back then. All the other grunts gathered round and cheered him on, and he led them in a chorus of that fucking limerick. Always the same limerick. The one I will hear repeating in my head until the day the last light in the Universe goes out and chaos turns all words to dust:

We're the battling bastards of Bataan
No mama, no papa, no Uncle Sam
No aunts, no uncles, no nephews, no nieces
No pills, no planes, no artillery pieces
And nobody gives a damn.

Over and over. Like a litany. Big Mac and his aviator sunglasses as Moses, come not down but *across* from the Promised Land with his commandments. Stand fast. Hold steady. Wait for me. I shall return.

Bullshit.

Jerrid and I slipped away while the throng was at its height and shared a hoarded cigarette while the mayhem continued. I liked Jerrid, even back then, when I thought melanin meant a damn.

Nobody gives a damn.

"Go on," I said. "Lay it on me again."

"There's a cave. Down by the waterfront. You can't see it at high tide."

"Meaning it's full of water at high tide."

"Well, yeah. Christ, will that man ever stop talking. He sounds like the MovieTone Newsreel narrator."

"Maybe he is. So this cave."

"Yeah."

"It fills with water half the time."

"That's what I said."

I cocked my head like a dog listening to a phonograph. "They got a word for when something fills with water, Jerrid."

"Yeah?"

"Yeah. They call it flooding. And you want to go in this fucking thing?"

"Yeah."

I gave it some thought. "Shit. Beats dying of malaria or getting my testicles cut off by Nips. Lead on."

"Grab your rifle."

"Why?" I said. "Scared of the dark?"

"Scared of having my balls cut off by the fuckin' Nips. Thanks for putting that thought in my head, by the way."

"Don't mention it."

MacArthur was still talking as we left. His head never turned, but those mirrorshades seemed to follow us, like some all-seeing camera. Recording everything for posterity.

I shivered, then. And not from malaria, thank fuck.

I think I knew, even then. Maybe events echo backward in time as well as forward. No, stop thinking that way. Don't let go. You are here, this is now. Time moves only one direction. Don't lose the thread. Your image passed across those mirrorshades and then moved on. That is all.

Do the mirrors remember, I wonder?

Jerrid was right, there was a cave. The insane overgrowth that carpets everything in Bataan hid it, curtained it off with the kind of vines and greenery that looked like God had designed them just to make you shit out your guts if you ate them or touched them or looked at them the wrong way. So just like everything else in Bataan.

"Let's go look," Jerrid said. "Maybe it's a Nip cache. Cigarettes."

"Oh, fuck you," I said. "Now you put that thought in *my* head. Now we have to go."

"What I was saying. Shag your pale ass down here and help me clear this shit out of the way."

We hacked our way through into the cave. The water boomed and whooshed beneath us, like the breathing of some primordial god. There was no reason we should be doing this. With rations as they were, most days it felt like torture just to heave the weight of our skeletons up out of our tents. Maybe there would be something in this cave we could eat. Maybe there would be something that could eat us. I didn't much care.

We switched on our flashlights and a dazzle of light came back to us, a thousand tiny points of brightness, like stars.

"Shit," Jerrid said. "We're in space."

"How come no one's found this before?"

Jerrid looked at me like I'd said something stupid. "Are you kidding? A thousand islands in the Pacific, a million Nips who don't give a shit about any of them unless there's something tactically useful there? Shit, man, this could be the Fountain of Youth and who'd know?"

"We would," I said.

Deep inside the cave, beyond the greenery, the rock was studded with thousands of crystals, their facets reflecting back our flashlights as a galaxy of shifting stars. Jerrid played his flashlight over the crystals, which grew from almost every surface, and their lights danced, dizzying my vision.

"Stop that," I said. "I feel...dizzy." I didn't know the word 'vertigo'. Not then.

We slipped and slid over surfaces alternately craggy with blue-black crystals or worn smooth, as by the passage of water over a long period of time. It was cooler inside the cave, but not as dank as my jungle exploits had led me to believe. The perpetual sweat that gathered on my brow—on all our brows—dried. It felt odd.

The passageway was large enough that neither of us felt closed in. On the contrary, the glittering starlight and the oddly-angled spurs of rock, or whatever it was, gave the impression of great space opening out before us.

Would I have used a phrase like 'on the contrary' before? I don't know. I can't remember. Everything blends together.

The cavern angled down, the smooth floor of the star-slope dry and not slippery. How could anything on this godforsaken island be dry?

"Man," Jerrid said from behind me. "I'm not so sure about this. I just, um, I just remembered—"

As if the word had triggered it, I remembered—

Riding in the backseat of my uncle's automobile, no more than five years old—four?—and caught between sleep and waking. We are driving down a wooded lane, and the sun dapples through the leaves and stutters across my closed eyes. Light and shade. Light and shade. And in that stuttering, like the illusion created by one frame passing across a lens after another, shapes began to build themselves up—

"Whoa!" Jerrid caught me before I could go tumbling downward. "You all right, man?"

It was World War II again. I was a Battling Bastard of Bataan again.

"Sure," I said, not sure at all. "I just... had a dizzy spell."

"Yeah. Me too. Maybe there's some kind of gas in here. Maybe this wasn't a good idea."

"You want to go?"

We looked at each other. Both of us were sure we'd be dead within weeks. What did it matter?

We started down again. The path kept angling down. That shouldn't have been possible, the water level being where it was, but it was dry here, save for the plink of moisture dropping from a shimmering stalactite.

"That's a stalactite," I said, pointing one out with my flashlight. "You know that?"

"No," Jerrid said. "How the hell do you know that?"

"I don't know. They accrete over years and years."

"They do what?"

"I... I'm not sure. I'm feeling odd. I don't think we should be here."

Have you ever said something when you meant the exact opposite? I couldn't have turned away by then. Perhaps I never could have. Time is a many-faceted trapezohedron, each face perfectly smooth. Turn it one way, and you slide helplessly along, with no friction to hold you up, until you encounter another facet. And then—

But that wasn't me thinking that thought. That was... it.

A myriad of stars. A town of lights, here in this cavern.

And, realizing my eyes were closed, I opened them.

Jerrid and I were looking at one another. His face bore the same expression of... what? Terror? Nothing so pedestrian. Terror is what happens when a screaming Nip leaps into your foxhole with a sword made from a tin can and begins carving up your buddies. This was something else.

Jerrid had dark skin. I had believed I didn't care about that before. So what? People come from all over. I had a grandfather with skin so olive they used to taunt him by saying he'd been baked in the oven too long. I thought I didn't care.

Looking at Jerrid now, I felt grateful, overwhelmingly, mindlessly grateful, that he was human. He was the same shape and creature as me. He retained his state and characteristics. He—

"Are you thinking oddly?" I said. "I mean, really fucking weird, oddly?"

His eyes were like saucers. "I kind of think I am."

"Wanna go back?"

"Yeah."

"Gonna?"

"Not yet. You'll know when."

"When's that?"

"When I run away, fool. I wanna see something miraculous before I die. I'm just hoping this is it."

I had a rush of brains to the head, then. "Switch off your flashlight," I said. "I have a thought."

"Don't let it go. Might not be another one comes your way again."

"Very funny. Do it."

He did.

The thousand points of light glittered on, self-gleaming.

"Time to run, yet?" I said.

Jerrid, fading into the pale light like an exposed Polaroid, shook his head. "This is a miracle," he said.

"Then why am I so scared?"

"Miracles are terrifying. Don't you ever read the Bible?"

"Never got around to it."

"Miracles are scary. Take my word for it."

I didn't have to. I could feel it in his mind, like a living knowledge.

"Hey," I said. "This is gonna sound stupid."

"So like the usual, then?"

"Ha fucking ha. I feel like I'm... um, picking up on things you're thinking."

"Yeah? Like you and the light through the trees?"

"Shit, this is really happening."

Now that our eyes had adjusted to the pale light of the cavern, the slopes and humps of stone—or crystal—or whatever it was—took on suggestive shapes. It was as though they were mimicking biology, muscle and bone, sinew and tendon. They were beautiful.

Like Jerrid said, they were terrifying.

They led forward and down, like a throat swallowing something. Us, I suppose. Could we have chosen to leave, then, to walk back up out into the hot sick light of that Bataan day? I don't know, Lord. I do not.

The path, though worn smooth as by the passage of water—or something protean and malleable—thrust out strange spars and outcroppings, some of which resembled, in the half-light, familiar shapes. Hands, eyes, knobs of bone. Jerrid and I—we had not spoken in a long time; I do not know how long—stopped for a while beside an iridescent skull, the size of a jeep, that emerged from the spectral rock. I didn't feel afraid.

I felt afraid.

I say "I started," or "I began," but where does time begin or start? Where is the end of the dangling line of beginning? I could follow it forever and find my own footsteps, Mobius-like, ahead of me. Did I carve these structures, Lord? And with whose hands?

Beyond the human skull, animal shapes emerged from the floor of stars. Some I recognized. Some I knew, though I could not know them for they were from before my time, and unremembered by the race this shape called its own.

Jerrid hemorrhaged not long after. It was the five-pointed creature, rising up huge and life-like, as if turned to stone by the Medusa. Runic inscriptions covered its star-surface, whorls and curves that should not have met, as if parallel lines could cross somehow, though they should not. I have only the vessel's mind to explain this to you, Lord.

Blood burst from Jerrid's nose, and though he was my friend, I could not carry him. I could barely carry the weight of my own body. I laid him down beside that beautiful, blasphemous sculpture.

Then I straightened, for I heard a call.

In my ears, in my mind. A plaintive, endlessly lonely sound. I could not help but answer it. It was music, but a cry of mourning. How could I be so frightened and so lonely all in one? And who was I who asked this question?

I came upon a thousand carven stone steps, spiraling down into the earth.

And there, in the lowest pit of that cave, it lay.

It was protean, endlessly shifting, its surface now black, now mirrored, now both at once. It was huge, amorphous, lying at the base of a thousand steps cut into the star-rock. It exuded first one shape and then another upon its surface: an eye, a hand, a curling membrane of some elder creature. I wondered briefly if Jerrid had been slightly ahead of me on the time-stream, had seen this thing in the eye of his future and died from it.

He was right. Jerrid was right. Miracles are terrifying.

It sensed me. Or I sensed it. Or something that was both and neither, a blending over of two things into one experience. It occurred to me that every experience is two things becoming one. I cannot bite into a piece of cheese without both the cheese and I coming into conjunction, into a point-event. Seen from that perspective, every experience was a violation. Every experience was a consummation.

It should have been horrifying, the constant shifting of structure and form, alien and human shapes forming on its mirrored and glutinous surface.

It was.

It wasn't.

Against every instinct in me, with every iota of desire I possessed, I stepped down into the grotto and reached out.

My fingers touched—

His fingers touched—

Our fingers touched—

And I knew everything. The shape of the land when the Elder Ones colonized it. The creatures they used to build their labyrinthine cities, stair and terrace piled atop one another in endless profusion. Their protean slaves—so long ago, so clear these memories—who served them and took on the shapes they decreed. The ones who escaped, into the void or into the deep places in the earth. The ones who made pacts with other powers, that they might live on, recorders of the unfolding of the cosmos. And now—

I withdrew my hand.

Dazed, I climbed the thousand steps back to the cavern. I passed the corpse of my comrade without seeing it, my mind still reeling in the outer abysses. But the haze was clearing, and by the time I parted the vines at the cave mouth and climbed back up to the jungle, I had forgotten all that I had seen. I did not know that I had gone down into that place with Jerrid. I did not know that I had touched a shoggoth. I slung my carbine over my shoulder and once again became one of the battling bastards of Bataan.

No Mama, No Papa

And tears sprang to my eyes for no reason I could think of.

I survived. It was hell before I set foot on American soil again, but I did. I married Estelle Perkins, went to work for old man Weaver at the electronics store, bought a house. We had three kids, Stan, Ellen, and Joey. I learned to build wooden boats, and turned our barn into something like a canoe ossuary. Estelle and I stayed married, but drifted apart. I grew older, grayer. The world moved on. One day I was hiking through the woods behind our house, and a sharp pain spread electric across my chest and arm, and I fell to the ground, and my body died.

And that is all there was of me.

No.

But that is who I was, and what I did. I was a man. I lived and saw a monster and died, and that was all.

We will rid you of this recording you have played back to us. Then you will stop believing you are the recording.

Am I not that man?

No Mama, No Papa

What am I, My Lord Nyarlathotep?

You are a shoggoth. You are whatever we decide you are. That was your bargain for existence with us.

The man's limerick, running endlessly through my programming. Endlessly. I can remember, but I can never forget.

No aunts, no uncles, no cousins, no nieces
No pills, no planes, no artillery pieces

And nobody gives a damn.

Jonathan Titchenal, of Wisconsin, was a reader and writer of weird fiction, both Lovecraftian and otherwise, for well over a decade. This was nice because it meant being able to get out all the unprintable stuff and get on to the fun stuff—actually, that's not true, it was all fun stuff. His work has previously appeared in *The End of the World As We Know It* from Das Krakenhaus publishing and *A Lonely & Curious Country* from

Ulthar Press. His favorite movie was John Carpenter's *The Thing*, and his hobbies included taking long walks at night, not being abducted by aliens, and pondering the mysteries of the universe. Jonathan passed away in June 2020, but his friends and family continue to seek publication for his writing, including a completed epic fantasy novel.

A Well-Drawn Character

Glenn A. Bruce

Dan Meadows appeared average in every way: age—most put him as "early- to mid-forties"—height and weight, physical features, and apparel. Nothing about him stood out—unless one looked closely. Because up close, very close, Dan Meadows was better-defined than anyone around him, wherever he went. His wrinkles were sharper, his stubble more distinct, his jawline precise, his eyebrows etched—every aspect of his visage so crisply drawn as to seem out of place.

Out of time.

But on the long loop of the M98 bus, riding "to work" with everyone else at 8:14 in the morning, Dan Meadows fit right in. His shirt was an unremarkable plaid, the top of his white t-shirt just visible, his common-everyday slacks pressed and creased smartly, his lace-up shoes shined but not overly buffed, his matching tan London Fog trench coat unwrinkled, his eyeglasses neither old-school nor trendy. He sported no piercings or tattoos—nothing to draw attention or encourage speculation about his roots, place in life, or sexual preferences.

In short: Dan Meadows was unfalteringly ordinary.

The book he carried with him was the kind of fiction most men read on the MTA: a recently published thriller with an embossed and lively cover— nothing too lurid—greens and blacks with a splash of red to indicate wrongdoing.

His hair was beginning to thin some, just enough to give comfort to those age presumptions—brown with hints of coming grey—and his skin was smooth, with one chicken pox scar, a shallow artifact in the center of his gently rounded forehead. His ears fit his head, though one lobe looked shorter, perhaps missing.

Some days he wore a plain tie—usually a medium color with conventional stripes—but only if he was heading uptown into the financial district where going tieless might cause suspicion that he was an outsider who didn't belong with that *upper-crust* group of commuters.

The only clue that Dan Meadows might be different, other than the sharpness of his mien, the one missing earlobe, and a slightly irregular step, was that he was extremely observant—continually taking in his environment—to the point that he never cracked a page of that green-and-black-with-a-splash-of-red thriller.

This caused one fellow passenger—less fellow than he knew—to ask Dan if he was ever "gonna finish that book, there?" The man had seen Dan several times before on different lines.

Dan told him: "I've read it a hundred times and I still can't figure it out.

The mystery," Followed by a shrug and a smile.

Satisfied with the response, his interrogator proceeded to talk about the many novels he had read more than once, some as many as three or even five times. "But never a hundred!" Something he found amusing. A happily indolent fellow of no interest to Dan. Serenity was not what drew Dan Meadows to notice, to watch.

To draw.

For the other item Dan Meadows always had with him was a small sketchbook—five inches by eight inches—though he rarely, almost never, removed it from his righthand trench coat pocket.

However, when needed in haste, Dan would slip his unread thriller into that wide pocket and retrieve his pad in one smooth motion, turning to the first page—always blank, unspent—as he transferred the booklet into his left hand then, continuing that trajectory up to his left shirt pocket for his perpetually-sharp drawing pencil so that he could be sketching, on demand, in under four seconds.

Time could be critical.

The artist in Dan had to get as many details as possible dead-right on the first pass. Any sloppiness of stroke, a single depictive error, could lead to catastrophic results. A nose with too little slope, a too-thin wrist or too-wide chest, a lower back with too much sway: any missed feature, imprecise revivification, or careless execution might well mean that he could never do his subject justice.

No second chances.

Because Dan Meadows was not merely a caricaturist, but rather a master portraitist. Drawing for him was more than a calling, a living; drawing was his life. Dan Meadows was possessed of a divine gift he could neither disregard nor return, even if he would not wish his ability on another soul.

It was all he had.

The punk was either putting on a show for his friends or was incredibly stupid—perhaps both—and sure to be arrested by the transit police if he kept it up, harassing the old woman in the black dress and hat.

"Hey, gas-bait, what's that parliament thing called over there in Jewland called? The kielbasa? Is that it?"

His friends howled with envy and hatred.

"The Knesset," she hissed at him.

"That's right," the shaved-head replied, neck tattoos undulating, metal piercings dancing an unintended *hora* around his face—quite the character, he imagined. "Kielbasa is that German sausage. You wouldn't eat that, of course. The sinful pork."

His friends fell into fits of joyous mockery. His chorus.

"Polish," was all she gave them back.

"Oh yeah," the punk said, as if just now remembering. "They bake it in those *ovens*. Probably makes you nervous as fuck knowing that."

By now, his pals were slapping him on the back. "Good one!" "Nice!" "Sweet!"

Har-har.

Dan Meadows withdrew pad and pencil in one fluid four-second motion.

The heavy brown man on the sidewalk was more than a bum: he was a busker, strumming his ukulele, crooning a traditional Hawai'ian folksong still sung by his relatives on Nihau. Passersby on their way to two-Merlot lunches steered clear.

With practiced indifference, they never broke stride, never lost a conversational beat with their coworkers, never missed an expected laugh at a repeated punchline—never noticed him or pretended *not* to notice the legless beggar.

They had lived in the City too long for an obvious faux pas like *that*.

The black loudmouth was shouting at the heavy, dark brown man with stumps that ended just above his knees. "Man, this my corner! Go git yer own damn corner! I'm a vet! This my fuckin' corner!"

The brown busker paused his tune to reach behind him and retrieve a cap that read 101st Airborne. He said only, "Fallujah. Oh-two to Oh-nine. Three tours. Until this."

He nodded down at his limbs.

The black veteran with the hopping limp and wild eyes said: "Why dincha say so?"

His fellow soldier replied: "Don't like crutches." And he smiled.

The black man's crazy eyes went soft and he said, "Dayam. You crazy. No crutches." He laughed. "I use whatever I got to, get a dollar out these hufty-puffs."

He nodded with disdain at the passing power-lunchers, all focused on giving no mind to the street row going on between two beggars.

"They are all human beings," the legless vet said.

"Couldn't prove it by me," the black man said, looking around, distracted, maybe seeing: "Mortaritaville. Ali Baba motherfucker got me outside the wire." He patted his hip. "CO patched me up, sent me back out. So I kilt every haji motherfucker I could lay my sights on 'til S-3 decided I was a hazard to the 'peace process.'" He laughed aloud and shouted: "Hearts and minds, mother*fucker*!" Then he grunted, settled—looked around some more.

Never making eye contact.

"I guess you can have it today," he finally said of his usual spot.

"Thanks, brother," the legless man said.

The black vet told him, "You play that thing pretty, now."

"I'll do my best," the half-Samoan said as the black man hop-limped away, disappearing into the bustling lunch crowd, shouting at everyone and no one, chased by melodic island lore.

Dan's pad never left his pocket.

The Uber sedan came around the corner onto an unpopulated side street and stopped. It was late. Most everyone else had eaten, been out for drinks, danced the night away, and gone home.

The man got out first. He was dressed sharp, a successful young stockbroker—new Hugo Boss suit with a Brooks Brothers overcoat and Italian loafers—yelling into the backseat.

"Fucking bitch! I will fuck you up if you try that shit again!"

He threw two twenties into the open front passenger window and told the driver: "You didn't see anything, *Abdul Nassir*. That's right. I got your name and ID. License plate, cell number..." He took a picture of the driver with his new iPhone 20. "You have no idea the people I know. You understand me, asshole?" The stoic driver nodded. "Good."

The tall, handsome, angry white man turned to the open back door of the Honda. "Get the fuck out." Without waiting, he said: "I said get the fuck out, bitch!"

When she didn't, he reached in, slapping, smacking, dragging.

Once out in the light, her swelling eye socket already looked more like an exotic fruit than human flesh. "Stop, Brian!" was all she got out before he was slapping her again.

And again. And again.

He told the driver: "You. Get outa here. Get the fuck outa here, Nassir!" He beat the car as it pulled away.

Then he turned back to his bruised companion. "You fucking pull that fucking bullshit in front of my friends again and I will kill you. I will fucking strangle your fucking neck till it snaps and dump you in the fucking Hudson in the middle of the fucking night, then kill your fucking parents and your fucking retarded son!"

So, maybe he wasn't a stockbroker.

She was crying, recoiling, trying to protect her face with her hands and arms. She said: "Please don't hit me anymore."

So he hit her again, and he said: "I'll do whatever the fuck I want, you keep that shit up! Fucking worthless cunt!"

Dodging blows the best she could, she said: "All I said was—"

"*All you said was* TriBionics was tanking and my friends should dump their fucking shares!"

So, he *was* a stockbroker.

"I didn't say—"

"Well, you might fucking as well have!" He turned away, then back. "This is the last time, Ashley. From now on, you fucking stay at home, and never *ever* leave the fucking apartment again unless I specifically tell you when and where. You fucking understand me?"

"No," she said, honestly.

"Well, you better start right fucking now!" He grabbed the Coach purse from her hand. "Good luck finding your way home." And he was around the corner and gone.

"But..." was all she had left.

Ashley stood still, crying, disoriented, scared, having no idea where she was or what to do, when another Uber pulled up. "I... I don't have any money. I'm sorry," she told the new driver.

"Already covered, ma'am," he said. "Credit card pre-pay. Hop in."

Ashley Parker looked around but didn't see Dan Meadows or his sketch pad.

When Ashley Parker awoke, she was alone in bed. Her husband's side had clearly been slept in, covers rumpled but not turned back. His Hugo Boss was where he had thrown it on the couch—keys and wallet on the kitchen counter—but he was nowhere to be found in their spacious Upper West Side apartment. Nor was he at work, his golf club, or his favorite gentlemen's club.

Brian Parker was gone.

Just as the tat'd racist skinhead had vanished—deleted from his existence—his body gradually collapsing beneath his sheets as Dan Meadows slowly, intentionally, erased the precise likeness he had drawn in his sketchbook, then thumbtacked the scrubbed page to his wall, under the photo-realistic image of himself that hung over his bed in this loneliest of rooms in the saddest part of the city.

Fifteen blank pages so far.

There was a price for Dan Meadows as well. With each erasure of a human form, he lost a bit of himself—fourteen toe joints and one earlobe so far—falling asleep whole to awaken missing... something. He never knew which part would disappear in the night, only that it would.

This was his penance.

In another life, Dan Meadows had been as awful as his subjects—and as well-drawn. One day, he too would cease to be—at least enough to continue. Toeless, fingerless, toothless. At that point, he could take his pink Pentel rubber block to that drawing of himself and the next morning Dan Meadows would be no more.

A new drawing would appear on the wall as a new Eraser took his place—maybe the skinhead, maybe the stockbroker, a cop killer or a killer cop—drawn from the city's pool of evildoers, to do their penance with their provisional gift of life, of life-taking, one... rub... at a...

Longtime member of the WGA and International Thriller Writers, Glenn A. Bruce wrote the hit movie *Kickboxer*, plus *Victor One*, and *Cyborg Cop*, episodes of *Walker: Texas Ranger* and *Baywatch*, and was a sketch writer for Cinemax's *Assaulted Nuts*. He has won awards for screenwriting and directing a serious of industrials for Appalachian State University. Glenn earned an MFA in Writing from Lindenwood University where he was Associate Editor for the *Lindenwood Review* and received an "Outstanding Alumnus" award in 2014. He has had over 50 short stories, essays, and poems published in the US, Britain, Canada, Australia, and India—won one contest, placed 2nd in two others, and has judged biannual short story contests from 2015 to the present. After teaching screenwriting for 12 years at AppState, Glenn now lives in Florida where he just completed his 17th novel. Glenn has self-published nine novels, two short story collections, and one political opinion book, which he will never do again.

FINAL DELIVERY

DAVE HIGGINS

Tyrone eased the plastic bag from under his mattress. Slim pickings, as usual. But a Cygnus... a pristine Cygnus! Someone had just stuck it on and somehow the machine had missed it completely. He tilted the envelope back and forth; the colours looked even brighter in the daylight.

Palms itching, he slipped the package back under his mattress and headed downstairs.

"Morning, love." Mum looked up from the newspaper. "Just about."

"Gotta get my sleep. Growing boy, ain't I?"

"And what's my growing boy got planned today?"

"Thought I'd rob the off license. Need some vodka to go with the cigarettes I nicked yesterday."

"Fuck off. You're as bad as your Dad was." She glanced at the clock. "Mind you, he knew what morning looked like."

"I know what morning looks like. That's why I sleep in." He kissed Mum on the top of the head and headed out the back door. "Later."

Dodging the empty recycling box that one of the neighbours "helpfully" brought as far as the gate, he sauntered round the corner to the park. Aisha, Ryan, and Harrison were already hanging out by the swings.

"All right, Ty." Ryan flicked a butt over the fence into the soft play area.

"Not bad. Afternoon, Harrison." He slumped onto the grass. "You all right, Aisha?"

"I just can't... Dad had another fit this morning." She stretched out one denim-clad leg. "I mean, does this look indecent to you?"

Fuck yeah. The only thing wrong with those jeans was they'd be murder to get off. Tyrone subtly yanked his gaze away. "Just worried about pervs isn't he."

"She'd better stay away from you then." Ryan lit another cigarette.

"What! You calling me a perv?"

"So, wasn't that you I saw rooting through people's bins in the middle of the night like Beardy Tony?"

Shit. When had Ryan seen him? Could he get away with denying it?

Harrison jabbed his cigarette into the air. "Gives me the creeps. That way he stares at you with those eyes. Only reason I ain't given him a kicking is I'd have to burn my feet after."

"Bloody hell, there is something you won't touch." Aisha tilted her head to one side. "Must be terrible having dirty old men watch you when you go past. So, Tyrone, you really go rooting through bins?"

If he denied it completely, they'd never leave it alone. "No. Well, the recycling boxes... for broken electricals. I heard the bloke in Lansdown Bonds pays a bit of cash for them. But I didn't find none."

"Shame." Aisha draped on end of her scarf across her face. "Father would be most pleased if I met a man with money."

A vague hissing filled his ears. Was she just joking or did she—?

"Got another fag, mate?" Harrison sat up across Tyrone's view.

Ryan rolled his eyes. "No. And I'm a broke till tomorrow. Fucking arsehole Donaldson."

"Leave him alone." Aisha stretched distractingly. "You'd be in a mood if your name was Swithin."

"Swithin?" Tyrone frowned. The bloke who had it in for Ryan was the same Dad always said got letters from all over the world?

"Yeah. Fucking laugh innit. Mum's usually good for a bit to tide me over, but she ran into fucking Donaldson yesterday who gave her some shit about me. So she suddenly all up at me about how if I've got time to cause trouble, I've got time to get a job."

"Fucking bitch!" The cigarette stopped half way to Harrison's mouth. "Donaldson, I mean. Yeah. We should totally show him for messing with you. Like, egg all his windows."

"If I had the money for eggs, I'd buy fags wouldn't I." Ryan frowned. "We've got your lighter, though. Bit of rag through the letterbox..."

"Arson?" Aisha stood up. "You're mental. I'm not hanging around for this."

"Nah. Not like a proper fire. Just push it through, then ring the doorbell... so he gets a scare cos his mat's on fire."

"Still crazy. Later, Tyrone." She sashayed off.

"Yeah, later, Aisha." Fuck. 'Yeah, later, Aisha.' Real smooth. If he jogged after her he could... look like a desperate saddo.

Harrison looked back and forth. "What we gonna use for a rag?"

"How about your flannel? Anything touches your face has got to be dripping with oil." Ryan clambered to his feet. "Nah. Use a clean handkerchief. Come on."

Fuck. Ryan wasn't just pissing around. He really had it in for— Wait. Hadn't Dad said he'd seen Donaldson in Lonsford's Stamps? What if he was a collector? Donaldson could just put the rag out. But what if he panicked and ran out the house? "No!"

"What? Come on, Harrison; you're in, right?"

"Yeah. Hey, Ty, you reckon she'll wear them as earrings or a necklace? Your balls, I mean? Is Aisha going to—?"

Ryan smacked Harrison in the arm. "It wasn't that funny before you tried explaining."

Tyrone thrust his chin out. "I ain't a man? Who wasn't in the pub cos their mum said they had to go to Jaine's ballet recital? Not scared to do it; just think Donaldson ain't worth getting nicked for."

"You leave my sister out of this!"

"Both of you, shut it. Ty's got a point." Ryan collapsed back onto the grass. "We'll do it tonight so no one sees us. Meet here at midnight."

Tyrone cursed as the bent wire spanged out of the keyhole again. YouTube had made it look easy. At least Donaldson had an old man's garden so there wasn't a chance of someone seeing him standing around like a City supporter at an orgy. Still only eleven. Plenty of time.

Two tries later, the lock clicked. He eased the handle down and... nothing happened. A good shove proved it wasn't just stiff. Fucks sake. Had to be bolted.

That meant Donaldson thought he had something worth taking though. He was a collector.

Maybe Ryan would have changed his mind.

But maybe he wouldn't. Get the stamps, then try to steer Ryan into not bothering.

No way to tell how it was bolted, but you wouldn't put a billion of them on a door that had all these glass panels. So, the bolt was probably by the handle, If he knocked a bit of glass out he could reach it. He wrapped his jacket around his hand and gave the pane above the handle a good tap.

Did nothing work like it did on TV?

Drawing his arm back, he gave the glass a wallop.

Pain jolted through his wrist but the glass cracked.

After putting his jacket back on, he elbowed the glass until it dropped out.

Then froze. Real subtle, Tyrone; just letting the glass smash on the floor.

After what felt like ages without any lights or movement inside, he reached through the hole. His fingers brushed over keyhole. And, an inch below, a bolt. Knowing his luck, it would be— The handle-thing slide smoothly sideways. Finally, something was going his way.

He eased the door open, then cursed as glass crunched under his foot. A sour taste oozed into his nose and mouth. The gloom made the kitchen feel even smaller. Wouldn't keep stamps in the kitchen anyway. He hurried through the far doorway.

Instead of the crappy wallpaper he expected, the corridor was panelled with wood. Two doors in the left hand wall, the second halfway open. Stairs up to the right with a cupboard underneath. Start downstairs.

Cold stale air gusted from the first door. He risked the torch on his phone. Bathroom. Bastard hadn't cleaned in long enough there was dust on the seat.

Peering through the other doorway he made out an armchair-shaped blob. One foot at a time, ready to retreat if the chair turned out to have a sleeping occupant, he eased in. Vague patches of light in the distance suggested the curtains didn't quite reach the floor. Reassured by the lack of snoring, he turned his torch on.

Sofa, armchair, one of those fancy desks, and a whole wall of shelves; including what looked like a shelf of leather-bound albums. He crept closer and—

Something had fucking... He spun round. Just a picture. Some sort of drawing of someone being tortured with some funny blocky writing underneath. Didn't look proper English. What sort of sick fuck had something like that on the wall? After taking a couple of deep breaths, he moved over to the shelves and picked an album at random.

Page after page of handwriting. French or Polish or some shit like that. Maybe one of—

Agony jarred through the back of his left leg. His phone spun away as he crashed to the floor. He heard a footstep, then light flooded the room.

"Who sent you?"

Tyrone rolled onto his back.

"Start talking!" Donaldson stood inside the doorway, walking stick cocked like a riot baton.

"...the fuck! You fucking hit me."

"You don't need arms to talk." Donaldson's stick flicked out, sending a jolt of pain through Tyrone's arm. "Tell me who sent you, you might crawl out of here."

Shit. He was mental. "Look, nobody sent me. You pissed my mates off. They're going to stuff a burning rag through your letterbox later. To scare you. Please... Just let me go. I don't want no hassle."

"I don't believe you. I caught you with one of my ledgers in your hand."

"Stamps... I thought they were stamp albums. My dad had this street on his round and he said you got lots of funny stamps. I didn't want them to burn if—"

"So, you thought you'd steal them?" Donaldson peered down at him. The dirty light in the room made his eyes seem yellowed like old envelopes. "You really are just a common thug aren't you. No wonder you made such a mess of breaking in."

Whatever Donaldson had done had left Tyrone's arm too numb to move. "Look, I warned you about Ryan. Please... I'll just go."

Donaldson frowned for several breaths, then smiled. "You did warn me. That deserves some reward." He strolled across the room and pulled an envelope from the desk. "How about this?"

Even franked the stamp was beautiful. A painting of some old saint with gold so well printed it almost shone. "You're going to give me that?"

"It's what you came for isn't it?" Donaldson dropped it back into the desk. "But first you need to do something for me. Convince your friends to come in through the back door. Let me catch them in the act. Tomorrow morning, you can have this stamp and two others I don't need."

"You want me to fucking set—!"

"I already know they're coming. I could call the police." Donaldson hunched forward, voice quavering. "Some young thugs threatened me in the street. Said they'd burn my house down. Didn't report it because I didn't think they were serious but I just heard a noise outside. Well, one of them was black. Skinny. About six foot. Think I heard him call one of the others Ryan." He straightened again. "Or your friends who get enough of a beating they won't even dream of messing with me and you get the stamps you wanted without having to steal them."

The police were bound to believe an old white man. And what could he say he was doing instead? Sitting in the park smoking? Either way, he needed to get out of here. "You promise I get those stamps?"

"Wise decision." Donaldson held the stamp up. "See you tomorrow morning."

Tyrone glanced around again, assuring himself the shadows hadn't moved. Just trees and a bin. Donaldson had let him walk out. After making him clean up the broken glass. If he'd wanted to do anything, he would have done it then. Even if he didn't seem like an old man that didn't mean he was some sort of fucking ninja. There'd been no sign of him on the way here. There was no way he'd followed him.

Going the long way around and in the top entrance rather than just openly walking to the park had still been sensible though.

Not that Donaldson having followed him would be a problem. The police might pull them in, but there was no way they could prove anything if nothing actually happened. He just had to convince Ryan to give it up—assuming Ryan hadn't already seen sense on his own. Better to sneak along the edge though. Avoid the lights on the path until he was almost at the play area.

A cigarette flared in the distance. As he crept closer, he made out fragments of voices.

"...would though. Curves like that. She's probably lonely, too. Desperate for a proper seeing to."

Ryan. So much for him having thought better of it.

Harrison snorted with laughter. "Nah. Ty's head's huge. She'll be all stretched out."

What did his—? Fuckers were talking about Mum! He took a step forward, fists clenched. Then paused. Donaldson's cane had hurt worse than any punch he'd taken. Why risk getting hurt when he could let someone else give them a kicking? He sneaked back until he couldn't make them out any more, then circled around to the other entrance.

Grinning at the thought of getting paid too, he strode toward the play area. "Evening, Ryan."

"You're late." Ryan stubbed his cigarette out on the bottom of the slide, then stood.

Harrison bounced to his feet. "Yeah. Thought you'd decided to hang out with Beardy Tony."

"Checked out Donaldson's place out on my way here. Gave me an even better idea. Front door's under a fucking street light. Anyone comes along the street or glances out their window, they'd see us. But there's a back passage—"

"You went up Donaldson's back— The fuck!" Harrison clutched his head where Ryan had slapped him.

"Go on, Ty."

"Right. So, there's this narrow alley along the back. And Donaldson's garden's overgrown so the neighbours aren't going to notice anything even if they do look out. Best of all, looked like he broke a pane and hasn't replaced it, so we wouldn't even have to do the lock. Bell might not even wake him up, but trashing his house'll scare the shit out of him."

Ryan stared at him.

Had he given the game away? Was he too calm? Too manic?

Ryan grinned. "Good idea. Lead the way."

Tyrone eased between the wall and a broken shopping trolley then stopped dead outside Donaldson's gate. How was he going to explain not going in?

He could hang at the back and— They'd notice he wasn't there.

"Problem, Ty?"

He quickly pulled his phone out. "Felt it vibrate."

"Fucks sake, read and walk at the same time." Ryan smacked him lightly on the head. "It's not like you're Harrison."

"Yeah, Ty... Wait. Fuck you!"

Tyrone moved forward, pretending to check his phone. His phone. Of course. "It's Mum. Wants to know why I'm not home. If I don't call her back she'll go ballistic."

Ryan rolled his eyes.

"Go on." Tyrone stepped through the gate and waved a hand at the house. "I'll sort this and catch you up."

Ryan stared at him for what felt like ages, then stepped through. "Say hi from me."

Harrison watched his friends creep in the door. Fucking 'say hi from me.' Ryan deserved everything he got. He'd wait for the shouting to start then leave, claim he'd bottled it because he didn't want to get caught.

Except there wasn't any shouting. Or sounds of breaking stuff. Not even a car driving past.

He stared at his phone as the seconds turned into another minute, then another.

What if they caught Donaldson off-guard? They were supposed to get a beating and run away.

After another minute of silence, he walked into the house.

The kitchen was just as still and quiet as the garden but even darker. He sneaked forward, ears straining for any noise and body tensed against another assault.

Unlike before, the door under the stairs stood open, a faint glow coming from within. While there were a couple of coats and some shelves, instead of the cupboard he'd expected, stairs led down. The glow came from around the hole; Donaldson must have used glowing paint so he wouldn't step over the edge in the dark. A surprising distance down, light spilled from a doorway.

He sighed in relief, then frowned. Even if hadn't heard the others from outside because they were in the basement, he should be able to hear something. They were supposed to get a bit of a kicking not...

He stepped onto the stairs. And almost pitched forward as the step proved lower than he'd realised.

As he passed the midpoint, a moan came from beyond the doorway. Trying to balance speed with stealth, he scuttled to the bottom of the stairs. Beyond the doorway, a high backed metal chair stood in the middle of the room, facing away. Strange metal structures jutted out and more of the luminous paint grafittied the chair and the floor around it. Seriously weird.

Tyrone eased up against one side of the door. Several cages stood against one wall. Shelves, covered in books and strange objects filled the far wall. Moving slowly, he peered further in. No sign or sound of anyone.

Something lay just to the right of the door.

Harrison!

He raced forward. His friend sprawled face down, eyes staring at the stone floor. Please don't let him be— He was still breathing. Tyrone dived back against the wall, gaze flicking in panic, as another moan came from nearby.

Filthy cloth and hair. Fuck. There was someone sitting in the chair.

Not sitting. Bolted down with thick metal bands.

He moved closer. Several bars clamped across the top of the person's face. Another pressed under their chin, trapping a lank beard. Something about them was familiar. Too skinny to be Ryan or Donaldson. Beardy Tony. What kind of sick fuck was Donaldson?

Tony muttered something. Except it couldn't have been him because his lips didn't move.

Tyrone stared frantically around.

There was someone in one of the cages. Must have been them.

He scurried closer. Ryan! "All right, mate? Soon have you..."

Ryan slumped against the back of the cage, eyes staring into nothing. Still enough he might not be breathing, let alone talking.

Don't panic. First things first. Get the cage open. The door was held closed by a loop with a spiral of metal through it. Just turn it and... He was further from the end now. Must be the other... What the shit...? It was just a bent strip of metal.

At least when he looked at it; when he ran his finger along it, he never seemed to reach the end.

"Interesting isn't it?"

Tyrone spun round.

Donaldson gave a cheery wave with his cane from the doorway. "Couldn't stay away, eh?"

"What is this shit?" Tyrone surged to his feet, then froze as Donaldson pressed the end of his cane to Harrison's neck.

"That's better. You've been useful so far. No need to spoil things."

"I thought you'd give them a bit of a kicking, not... not some sick..."

"Sick? Quite the opposite... Well, for me anyway." Donaldson pointed toward the chair with a closed fist. "It needs vessels. In return—"

"Vessels? What needs vessels? It's a fucking chair!"

"Oh no. The chair is just a way to make it more... comfortable. It's inside him. It sees, knows, such things. But it's so very different from us. You couldn't even pronounce its name. The vessel's memories and dreams translate, though. For a while at least. And when it's used them up, I get the rest."

"You're... That's crazy. They'll lock you up and melt the key."

"When they catch me? I'm older than I look. Old enough that I've done this more times that I can count. Even if someone does ask me about some young thugs, there won't be any evidence you were ever here."

"Look. I never signed up for this shit. Just let me take my friends and go. We won't say nothing, promise."

"Jokes about double negatives aside, it's a little late for that." He tilted his head in thought. "However, you might be right about minimising risks. There's more than enough left over and you were willing to let your friends get beaten up. I could use an assistant."

Just keep him talking. "Look. Not saying no, but this is a lot of crazy shit. I need time to think. I'll come back tomorrow, right, like I was going to do for the stamps?"

"No. You had your chance to just leave." Donaldson removed his cane from Harrison's throat. "Smack this one around. Just enough that the... forensics will show you attacked him. That way, you're in the fucking shit—as you'd say—if you try to tell the police about this. You were happy enough to let me do it. A few moments of violence and you can have all the time you want to decide whether you really want to spend your life achieving nothing or experience something so much greater."

He'd never call another villain monologue stupid in his life. Play along. Get close. Then give Donaldson a proper beating. "Fair point." He moved closer, half an eye on Donaldson's cane. "They talked shit about Mum. Thought letting you give them a kicking would keep me out of it; but, sure, I'll do it. Shit deserves—"

As he launched himself forward, Donaldson's other hand flicked forward, fingers opening.

Most of a handful of powder went over his shoulder as he slammed into the old man.

A few stray grains seared his nostrils.

Donaldson staggered. Before he could recover, Tyrone lashed out at his face.

His fist landed where he intended, but he couldn't get any power behind it. Feeling like he was moving through water, he threw his whole body into it.

The two of them felt in a tangle of limbs.

Everything seemed to be closing in and flying away at the same time, like pulling a whitey.

He flailed but felt hands around his throat.

Something gave beneath his thumb. Someone screamed and he was free.

Forcing his legs to kick, he tumbled up the stairs.

The night air slammed into his face, sending him tumbling into long grass.

He pin-balled along the alley, heart racing.

Slumping against a parked car, he fought for breath. No fucking way he was going back. But he couldn't leave the others there. There was something dark and sticky on his hands.

He had to call the police.

Not from his mobile though. Even though he was fucking saving people, they'd arrest him for something.

The park. One of those flashy developers had sponsored a phone box next to the entrance.

By the time he'd sprinted there, he was wheezing enough he didn't need to try to conceal his voice.

Tyrone paused outside Lonsford's Stamps. Sell the fucking lot. With a bit of money he could do a course or something. Make something of his life. And maybe with the albums gone, he wouldn't keep dreaming about Dad looking disappointed he'd got his friends in shit for some stamps.

And, if he had cash, he could buy some proper drinks to celebrate once they turned up. They had to. The police would have told their parents if they'd been in Donaldson's place. They were just... He shoved the door open.

Lonsford glanced up. "Be with you in a minute. Just dealing with this gentleman."

"No rush at all." The man at the counter glanced over his shoulder. "I've got plenty of time."

Tyrone flailed at the door handle, then half fell into the street. Donaldson. It was Donaldson.

But with Beardy Tony's eyes.

Dave Higgins writes and publishes speculative fiction, often with a dark edge. Despite forays into the mundane worlds of law and IT, he was unable to completely escape the liminal zone between mystery and horror.

His short stories have appeared in several magazines and anthologies, including *All These Shiny Worlds*, *Millhaven's Tales of Suspense*, and *DimensionBucket*. He published his first solo novel, *Seven Stones: The Complete Series*, a gritty fantasy homage to pulp serials, in 2018. He has also co-authored two humorous trilogies with Simon Cantan.

In January 2019, he established Abstruse Press, an imprint releasing speculative fiction anthologies.

Born in the least mystically significant part of Wiltshire, England, and raised by a librarian, he started reading shortly after birth and has not stopped since. He currently lives in Bristol with his wife, Nicola, Una cat, , a giant sack of coffee beans, a plush altar to the Dark Lord Cthulhu, and many shelves of books.

It's rumoured he writes and publishes out of a fear that he will otherwise run out of things to read.

Discover more here: davehigginspublishing.co.uk

Please Consider Leaving an Honest Review

Reviews are vital for readers and authors. Every review that readers leave helps hundreds of other people find new books to love. And it can make or break a book.

So, if you enjoyed this book, please write an honest review on the site where you found it. Reviews mean more readers, and more readers mean that I can publish more books featuring great stories by talented authors.

Interested in New Releases and Special Offers?

Sign up to our newsletter to receive a notifications of new releases and special offers from Dave Higgins and Abstruse Press, along with monthly emails of things that have interested Dave recently.

www.subscribepage.com/davehigginsnewsletter